Medina 2

By
Jullian Smallwood

ISBN: Softcover   978-1-9820-2916-6

E-Book   978-1-9820-2916-1

This BOOK is dedicated

to

ICERINE
SMALLWOOD
(My Grandmother...)

Since I can't kiss you in the flesh, I throw kisses at the sky. To honor you!

Chapter 1

The police department wasn't thinking about the drug game, in the hood. Is like they weren't thinking about crime. So, it seems. Of course, they were watching. They just let it seem that way. While all along they were waiting for something to happen. Or, someone to make a major slip up. In the game of cops and robber someone always make a big mistake or a dummy move. Someone always did and always will do. That wasn't hard to find in the hood. The police department banks on somebody making a stupid move. Well for the police investigation into the drug game. That had never stopped. Operation take back the streets was all about getting the drugs off the street. And putting the drug dealers into jail. The operation was up and running in full force. They had so many leads, so many ways to find out what was going on, on the streets. The undercover unit had been formed just to deal with the excessive drug problem. Officer Smith and his partner Office Nickels were promoted to the special crimes unit. With a bunch of leads, which came after busting many of the smaller fishes. They locked a couple of them up on daily bases. And they start singing like canaries'. As soon as they locked them up, the next day someone was there to take their place. That was the crazy part about it. That made it nearly impossible to know who was really in charge. It became very frustrating for the officers who were assigned to the case. To them, it was like fighting a never-ending battle, with the street, with the criminals. Even though they knew it was a challenging endeavor they had to face. They all knew this, when

they signed up to be in this
unit. Even though it was
challenging, most of their
thoughts was, hell, they're
not going out, without a
fight. That was the theme
of their unit. Because they
weren't about to quit.
Instead, the officers went
harder. Eventually, they
had come across someone,
out of nowhere, who had
vital information pertaining
to capturing an important
individual who was major

contributor in the drug trade. They began to receive information on catching one of the big fish in the drug game. Unfortunately, the lead, lead nowhere. So, until they get something that will stick. The mission continues. As many arrest they made. Nobody wanted to deal nor work with them. They got little to no information from the people they arrest, who had any type of connections.

Not even the residents of community wanted to cooperate with the police department. The reason why most people didn't want to help or get involved. Because, most people didn't want to work with Officer Smith. The average person in the neighborhood didn't even like that cop. So, to deal with him, nobody wants any parts of that. Let alone talk to him. When Officer Smith asks anyone any questions.

They looked at him, and kept on walking, right pass him. With little to, no help with the people of the community. They kept on pressing, trying to find new leads and evidence. Trying find anything out, in the drug game, is like trying to solve a great big puzzle. When it comes to the police, the puzzle will eventually be solved.

The police drug unit was receiving all types of pressure from all angles.

Not only trying to find suspects of interest, but also from the upper-brass from the department. With all the diversions and wild goose chases the criminals put the police unit through. The local criminal, thinks the cops don't have a clue on what's going on. And what they were doing. They thought the cops weren't paying any real attention to the activities that was going on, right up under their noses.

But the cops were closer than they could image. Way closer that what they thought. So, while some of them thought the cops were stupid, not knowing the cops is almost on top of them. For now, the saga continues, the show keeps on moving. All is well, in the daily game of cops and robbers. Somedays felt like it was a mad, mad world out there. Everybody knows something, yet nobody knows nothing.

During this time Ty laid-low and made money. While he made his daily rounds, he watched his moves to a tee. He avoids the attention as much as possible. That's why he hired people to take care of the dirty work.
Ty wasn't taking any chances. The only thing he continued to do, was collecting the money. He hired someone else to drop the drugs off to the spots. As he hustles to get

money. He made sure he took good care of himself. Everything he did was from far away as possible. At his day job, the union which he was part of decided to go on strike. They demanded a raise, and they wanted better benefits. The new owner of the company had a meeting with the heads of the union. The union said what they wanted. The changes they would like to see. The owner told them what he was going to offer them. The union said that was unacceptable. The owner said, take it or leave it. The union decided to go on with the strike. The owner continued to hold out until the union reps could come up with something better. The union had to explain to the workers why they felt like striking was the only way to get what they wanted.

The union rep. told the workers at their union meeting. The rep. wanted to get some feedback on how the workers felt about how everything was being dealt with. After a little back and forth, with ideas. The union rep. went back to management with a new package the union wanted from the company. The union agreed with management for an undisclosed amount to sign

the new contract, with
little to no changes on it.
So, the strike was over.
What the workers thought
they were going to get. To
what they actually, got
which was nothing. Their
next pay check proved that
fact. They did receive a
25-cent raise, that got
swallowed up in taxes. No
extra benefits. None of
the worker were pleased by
the results of their strike.
They union said that was

the best offer on the table. So, they had no choice, but to take the offer. The union rep. stated that it was not great, but it was better than what they had before. The word around the office was that it was better than nothing. Ty was totally disappointed with the union on this one. The only good thing out of all it was the union rep. did say, it was only a 1-year agreement. That was the only thing the union rep. said that made any sense. That meant he'll be back next year to renegotiate the contract. For the time being, not too many was happy at the work place. When Ty reached home after the union meeting he sat down and discuss the situation with Dana. Dana was stunned with what had taken place. She stood there, listening in disbelief. Ty felt some type of way about it. Because he hardly came home talking about work. Dana asks him, what was he going to do about it? He told her, he's going to do nothing, at the present time. He did say, he would be looking for another job. Right now, he has to do, what he has to do to take care of his family. With his job making him feel like he was at a dead-end job. That made him all the more eager to find a new job, something better. On the street side of the coin, after having a nice run of the drug operation. Just like all drug businesses, after dominating the weed game in his local area. Having a massive amount of territory. Most people in the neighborhood smoked weed, that they provided. If they knew they were, or if they didn't know, they were. When all is well in the streets hustling game. Competition eventually came. When your making money on the streets, people will be watching. Many of the people wanted in, on the action. The money, the finer things, the cars, all of it, was what everyone wanted part of. In a broke environment everyone wanted and needed. Some would do just about any and everything to get their hands on it. The money was very tempting to all. Like all things that goes on in the streets.

Sooner or later, individuals had to cross paths, bump heads. Whatever you wanted to call it. That's when the problems start to mount up. Then the after effect of problems, becomes street wars, onto violence which was enviable. When dealing with poor people needing money. In a matter of time the spot got robbed. Ty and his partners didn't know it was a random robbery. Or was it a personal.

Most people didn't know about the whole operation. Most didn't have the slightest clue on how to connect all the real dots. Then they thought about it, possibly it could have been an inside job. For now, all of that was just hear say. Not knowing was the biggest problem of it all. That's the question, that remained in the air. The question of who would've been bold enough to rob one their spots.

Especially their biggest spot, that brought in the most money. The spot they called the big house. Who really had the guts and balls to rob the big house. That's where they had most of their drugs and money at. The most popular spot by far. Ty took a major hit when they robbed the big house. Not only did they rob the joint, they shot the spot up. During the shoot-out, 2 of his workers got shot.

One got shot in his leg, the other got shot in the arm. The worst thing about it was one of the three workers got murdered, in the process. When that happened, that really made the spot super-hot. With the spot being on full blast. It became a total loss, for the moment. Police tape block off the spot. The only good thing that came out it was the worker who got murdered, got murdered outside in front of the spot. Not inside the spot. The body was moved, but the chalked outline of the body remained there for a couple of days. As well as the police tape. All Ty could do was shake his head, in totally disbelief. Someone who was there told Ty that one of his partners got killed. But Ty already knew that. Ty's attitude completely changed afterwards.

Now, he wanted to find out who done this, for real, for real. After checking out the scene, he headed over to the hospital to check on his other workers. When he got to the hospital the workers explained the story to him. They told him a couple of masked dudes came in the spot and robbed them at gun-point. When they tried to run away that's when the guys started shooting at them.

They got away with the
money and the drugs.
After they shot them, the
men hopped in a dark car
with no license plates.
Which made it impossible
to see who did it. Or, what
car they drove off in.
Later, that evening Ty call
a meeting to discuss what
had happened. All of them
wanted to seek some type
of revenge. The only
problem was they didn't
know where or who this was
coming from.

Ty got to the point, he told them, first thing first, they needed to find out who did this. And deal with it. While Ty was driving home, he began to think about it all. All of this was beginning to be overwhelming. The realization hit him, things were getting way out of hand. Unfortunately for Ty, he was way too deep involved with it all, to even think about a way out.

Even though he was contemplating on how to exit. He knew what he was into, was way bigger than himself. The oath he took on the streets, way back when. Brought him a lot of obligations. He had to hold too. To lead this syndicate, at least until Sparky comes home from jail. Until then many mouths had to be fed. It was always bigger than just one individual. That didn't mean that he was ready to put his life on the line for something petty, like revenge. Knowing everything has changed. What's next? No one knows! Only God knows that. Only God knows the outcome of it all. Ty just knew, if anything was to happen to Dana and his boys. He would lose it, go crazy. That's why he keeps his family far away from the street shit. He always moved the way he did on purpose.

At all times he made sure no one knew where Dana and his kids were at. Only a few, trusted individuals knew their whereabouts. Ty was getting his arsenal together. Just in case, if he had to go to war with another street crew. A street war wasn't in his plans. Also, he understood he could not afford to take a major hit, like the one that just happened. They had to make a move back, or everyone would think it's sweet to rob them. Their spots. An example must be made. It took them a couple of weeks, more like a little over a month to get the spot up and running again. This time they hired security to watch over the spot. Well you know, street security, more man-power. They needed the spot to be extremely secure. Also, they put up some surveillance cameras to see outside and inside of the spot.

Ty wasn't playing with that.
It was too much money
being made, to take
unnecessary risk. Ty knew
it was about to get real out
there. He wanted to be
prepared for it. That was
a fact. Dana began to get
very confused. She didn't
know how to act nor react
to Ty. Ty wasn't acting like
himself anymore. He
became distant and
different. Some days she
knew who she was dealing

with. The next day she felt like she was sleep with a stranger. At times she didn't know how to deal with it. She didn't tell anybody about the feelings she was having. So, she took it like it was a passing fad. Nobody, not even Ty knew. She was well aware, that one of his childhood friends just got murdered. Also, she knew that two other friends just got shot. She came to the conclusion, that was root of the problem. When she asks him, how did he feel, he told her, he's maintaining, and he'll get through this like any and everything else. Dana knew it takes time to go through life's situations. Dana loves Ty, no matter whatever he was going through in his life. All she wanted to do, was be there for him. That was her goal. Her plan. She knew Ty was let down some many times in his life.

Always losing people that he loves. Dana felt like Ty was always handed a short-end of the stick, in life. She didn't want to be a participant of that. After all, one his friends were murdered and two was shot. Of course, Ty got real with life. Because life got real with him. Sometimes he didn't even care anymore. Somedays he was unpredictable, unstable, plus unwanted.

All these thoughts races through his mind. He began to feel guilty for putting these guys, his friends' lives in these screwed up predicaments. The little bit of feelings he processed inside began to go haywire. To make matters even worst, at least half of his workers got locked up. And a nice portion jumped ship. They went to work for his rivals. In return, Ty had to take things into his own hands.

Working and hustling began to take its toll on Ty. He wasn't about to give his man-made enterprise. He's not giving that up without a fight. You can believe and put your money on that. Dana had enough things to worry about. In life, us human-beings act like we're in control. Truth be told, God is in control over it all. Us humans, just think we in control, in charge. With life, you can't always predict the outcome.

dealing with life, it is,
what it is, in life. While all
this was going on, Ty took
some well needed time off,
to spend time with Dana
and the boys. While he was
with his family Ty had the
time of his life. Ty and
Dana were finally able
to talk about what he was
going through. They both
wanted to have another
baby. They even discuss it.
They both agreed when
things got better, they
would plan it out.

Well, things don't always go as planned. Dana went for her yearly check-up. The doctor said she wanted to talk to her. She didn't know why? That made her puzzled. After she ran some more test, to make sure. She called Dana back into her office. When she got some results back from some of the test. First, she began by telling Dana that she was fine. Nothing was wrong with her.

She had no need to worry about that. Dana was relieved to hear that. Then she informed Dana that she was pregnant. Dana was at first speechless. Then she asks the doctor to take another pregnancy test just to make sure. The doctor agreed. Dana thought maybe they had made a mistake, or something. She wasn't expecting to hear that. She was completely shocked. She was surprised of the fact.

She was overwhelmed with emotion. She didn't know how to response to this. After the results came back, it was confirmed she was pregnant. With the results she received, she was stuck. Amazed with the fact. When she got home. She called Tanya and told her about it. They spoke on the phone for hours talking about it. Tanya asked Dana how was she going to tell Ty about it.

She told her, she really didn't care how Ty felt about it. Her only concern was how would they be able to afford this new addition in their family. Dana wanted this baby regardless. Dana really wanted a baby girl. She wouldn't have been mad, if she was going to have another baby boy. Dana was a strong believer in faith. Whatever God wanted it to be, will be.

She was hesitant to tell Ty the newly found news. When she finally had the courage to tell Ty. Ty was actually happy to hear the news. He told her, he hopes they were having a baby girl. He let it be known that's what he wanted. Dana reminded him that they didn't know what they were having at this point of time. Ty was happy outside, but deep down inside, he was a little stress about it.

He felt like he wasn't making enough money to handle a third child. He was making money, but not the way he really wanted to make money. He wanted to be more legit, than he was. As far as, his drug spots were going. At the time, he was actually losing more money than he was gaining. Ty did have a stash of money in the bedroom closet. He had 50,000 dollars in a suit case.

He was saving the money for a rainy day. Once a point in time, Dana and Ty's relationship was vibrate and natural. It was special, free willed, unique filled with love. The feelings were still there. Just not as strong as it once was. No, question about that. Now, they're about to add another edition to the element. Yes, Dana was happy with Ty's new-found love for her and kids.

Still, in the back of her head, deep in her thoughts. She was getting prepared for something else. Something she knew not, what it was. Maybe it's a warning of the time. Woman's intuition, maybe that was the case. She felt like, who is she to question how she felt inside. When it came down to her heart, mind and soul. She knew, she loves her man. She was certain about that.

Right now, she's pregnant and going through all types of emotions. All she knew was that she wanted to have a healthy baby. Her stressing herself out, isn't going to help her nor the baby. What Dana thought was a one-time thing with Ty and the law. The reality of it all, was that turned out, not to be true.
Because on the other hand, Ty became a magnet to the law.

Ty and the law became like shit to flies. No matter what he did. Trouble followed right behind him. Once upon a point of time, he was two-steps ahead of the game. Now it felt like he was just a single step ahead of the law. Ever since he didn't have his right-hand man anymore. Omar got sentenced to 3 years in prison. O got caught at the wrong place, at the wrong time.

In the hood, Ty was fully aware that he only could count on himself. He knew, he had to hold himself down. These new people he had around him, couldn't be trusted. The people he did trust, vanished into thin air. Disappearing like they never existed in the first place. Because of the fact, every time, whenever he made any type of drug transaction. He made sure, he was packing a pistol.

Feeling alone in a game that doesn't love anyone. The streets were always watching. One false move, the streets was there to swallow you up. Most of the time, if not all the time, there's no happy endings to any movie of a hustler. Just when Ty forgot about Police officers Smith and Nickels and the law. The law and the officers didn't forget about him. Nothing was new with that.

Whenever, Officer Smith saw Ty, he made it his business to give Ty a hard time. Most of time, he found nothing. But it was also the time he found what he was looking for. This time Officer Smith had hit the jackpot. When Officer Smith put his patrol car sirens on. He instructed Ty to pull his vehicle over. Ty looks, into his rear-view mirror.

He saw it was Officer
Smith. All he could say
after that, was Damn.
Ty realized then, that this
day, was not his day. Ty
already knew the game was
over. When the Officers
checked Ty's car. They
discovered a pound of weed
in it. When they searched
him, they found a firearm
on his waist. They found a
9mm gun, On his waist
band. Police Smith took the
firearm from Ty's waist
and looked at him and said,

"What is this?" smiling as he spoke. Ty already knew the outcome. He knew because he got caught dirty, red handed. The outcome was of course, Officer Smith arrested him immediately, right on the spot. The look on Officer Smith and Ty's face was priceless. Both of them, felt a certain way about it. Only they knew what they were thinking at that point in time.

Ty definitely, had some
words about it. And none
of his words were very
nice. Ty was pissed off
about the whole situation.
This time Ty went through
the whole system. This
time around the judge
remanded him. After going
back and forth to court,
within a six-month period
of time. Every time he
went to court, Dana was
sitting there in the
courtroom, in support.

They were able to see one another for a moment. Then the case was settled. Ty had no other choice, but to take a plea deal. He took what they offered him. 3 years was the offer on the table. Dana sat in the courtroom that day of sentencing. She sat there with her sister. She began to weep about the whole situation. As the tears ran down her cheek bones. She began to rub her belly.

She sat there shaking her head beyond pissed off with Ty. After he went away. She traveled a few times to see him while he was on Riker's island. When he got shipped up-north, they both agreed she shouldn't travel that far due to her pregnancy. At first, she felt bad for him. Then the realization came into play. She took it for what it's worth. She realized, she didn't know the half of what he was doing out there. That really bothered her. She began to go through a whole wild wind of emotions. She really didn't know what to tell her family. Not even what to tell her kids about the whereabouts of Ty. She started off trying to cover it up. For a while, it worked. Most of the summer to be exact. Finally, she had to come clean about it. She had no choice in this matter.

She remained working at her job. She asked and got more hours on her job. She was doing hair on the side, on weekends. She also began to use the money that Ty gave her, that she had saved. Ty didn't know this. But most of the time, when he gave her money, she wouldn't spend much of it. The money she was saving behind his back turned out to be a pretty penny.

Also, Ty had that 50,000 in the suitcase hidden in the closet. In their bedroom. All together that was enough money to get her through a short period of time. It was okay for the time being. Once the money ran out. She really didn't know nor planned for the next move. That was the problem. She wasn't making that much at work, to begin with. She only had a part-time job.

When the secretary, who she was the assistant of, retired. She was offered the job. That was a major break for Dana. The doctor too, was very old in age. The doctor liked the way Dana worked and carried herself at his private practice at the local clinic. He was very impressed with the way she acted. He gave Dana her own assistant. Dana accepts the position.

She worked as long, as she could during the rest of her pregnancy. When she went on maternity leave. Her assistant took over the work in her absence. The kind old doctor reassured Dana that when she was ready to come back, her job would be there for her. She didn't have to worry about that. Her job was secured. Dana was extremely grateful for that. Even though, so much more was going on.

She really needed the job
and the money. So, she
was happy about that. That
contributed to her being
humble and thankful.
She always felt blessed,
highly favored in the eyes
of God. The day came, the
day Dana gave birth to her
third child. Her third baby
was a baby girl. What she
dearly wanted. She had a
beautiful, healthy baby
girl. She named her
Myesha Medina. Dana was
excited in all.

Still she was feeling a type of way because Ty wasn't there. She didn't feel alone. Her mother and Tanya were there to be by her side. When Ty called from prison. Dana wasn't home. She was at the hospital with the baby that she just had. Her sister answered the phone. Her sister was babysitting the boys for Dana. Her sister told Ty that she had a baby girl. Then she told Ty congratulations.

Ty told her sister that he said he was happy about their new addition to their family. He also asked when Dana got a chance, could she send him a picture of the new baby? Ty hung up the phone. His phone time was up. Ty was happy as can be, in his predicament, as possible as he could be. The following day Dana was able to come home with the baby. Her brother picked her up from the hospital.

She didn't have to wait that long for her ride to come. He came, and they were on the route to Dana's place. When she got home, she was greeted by a bunch of friends and family. They all wanted to show their love and support for her. Dana felt the love. Which she really need at this stage of her life. It felt good to her. Still, she didn't know how to respond.

So, as Dana was known for.
She began to cry, tears of
joy. W.B. asked his mother
why she was crying for?
She told because she was
happy. He really didn't
understand. She knew that
by the look on his face.
She grabbed him and gave
him a hug. He didn't know
what to do. He hugged her
back. Dana sons was happy
to see her. While she was
away they were missing
her.

By this time everyone took turns holding the baby. Even Lil Ty held his new little sister. W.B. was 7 years old now, he wanted to hold the baby too. When Dana said no, not yet to him. He became upset. She told him, he could touch her, but not hold her. Dana noticed that W.B. was feeling left out of the process. That made him feel sad. She sat next to him and explains it a little more him.

A way so he could understand. She told him, wait until she gets a little bigger. Then he could hold her as much as he wants. He understood and agreed with his mommy. She was happy with that fact, she saw trades of W.B. being a great big brother to his little sister. When she was making dinner for her and the boys. Dana would take Myesha out of her playpen.

She held her baby in her arm, as she stirs the pots with the other hand. While she was doing, what she was doing. She began to talk to her baby girl. she vowed, that she will make her proud, no matter what it takes. They will be alright. They will make it. After the dinner was finished. Dana fixed the boys a plate. She called them to the kitchen. While she fed the baby her bottle.

After the baby finished
her bottle. Dana made she
burped. Then she places
her, in the baby high
chair. Dana ate a little.
She got the kids ready for
bed. Then she went to bed
also. Dana had access to
Ty's car. She refused to
drive it. She didn't know
what type of madness Ty
had got into, while driving
that vehicle. What she did
instead was she placed a
for sale sign on the car.

She figures that she'll sale it to the highest bidder. That would be the offer she took. Dana had a driver's license. She wanted to buy a cheaper car, than what Ty already had. What she was planning to do was sale the car, get something cheaper, then have enough money left over, to pay off the car insurance for the year. Which turns out to be great for her.

She didn't have to worry about that bill. Dana didn't stay on maternity leave for very long. The main reason was she needed the money. Basically, she couldn't afford to stay out of work for a long period of time. When her body got its strength back. She was ready to return to work. Thanks to her mother and her niece. Ms. Medina was about to retire at the end of the year.

She accumulated so much time on her job, time that she didn't use. She had plenty of time to take off, now and then. When she wasn't watching the baby, her niece was. They made their schedules to fit babysitting for Dana. Ms. Medina took the days off that her grand-daughter had to attend her college classes. Everything fit right into place. Dana was grateful and thankful for the help.

She was so happy to be
back at work. She was
fully aware that somebody
had to pay the bills.
Thanks to God. God made a
way for her, to at least
maneuver, with what she
had to do. Dana's faith in
God grew stronger. She
was learning how to live and
survive without Ty. The
money she had, she uses it
wisely. She uses it, only
when she needs to. Things
for the kids that was
necessary.

Plus, she uses it for life's basics needs. Ty called like he always did, once a month. Ty told Dana, thanks, for sending him a picture of the baby. He also told her that their baby was beautiful and full of love like her mother. He let her know when he received the picture of their daughter, that made him realized he should be out of jail. He's supposed to be out there helping to raise his children.

He wanted his freedom. Just like everybody else who was in prison. He wanted to leave this hell hole, he found himself in. All he wants to do, was to touch his baby girl for the very first time. That's when it really hits him hard, where he was at. What's going on outside, he had no control over. The fact of the matter, he was on ice. All he knew, was he damn sure didn't want to be in this joint.

He places the picture of Myesha on the wall of his prison cell. Somedays all he did was just stir at his baby girl's picture. He stirs at the picture, until the lights went off on the pier where his cell was on. Dana was able to weather the storm. 2 years passed, like it was a short time frame. Dana was able to maintain on her own. She felt good and proud about that. She made great strides.

After serving a 3-year bid, Ty was released on parole after 2 years. Ty and Dana kept in contact, all through his jail time. Even though many people in her life told her, not to do so. Many thought it wasn't good idea. But, no one could do anything about that. Nothing could stop Dana from taking Ty back. The first thing he did when he got home, he went to see his daughter.

Ty's eyes were wide-open, when he laid his eyes on his baby girl for the very first time. A special moment for him, was when he was able to hold the baby for the first time. Moments like that were priceless. Tears were in everyone's eyes, who witnessed it. Ty looks at Dana and promises her that he would not be going back to jail again. Ty explains to Dana, he wanted a chance.

A chance to start over. He tells her, he wants to start all over again, with her and the kids. The family he helped create. When he came home at first, no one wanted to hire him. The struggle was on, and it was for real. Most places didn't want any parts of someone who was on parole. He had to check in, once a month to see his parole officer. He had to do random drug test, the whole works.

He still had a little bit of money on the streets. But nowhere near the kind of money he was getting before. Most of the crew, he started out with, was either dead or in jail. Or they went legit. They didn't want to be bothered with the game, anymore. Nobody couldn't blame them either. Including Ty, he knew and understood what they were saying.

Especially the fact, they weren't getting any younger. Ty knew, but for him, he found little to no opportunities for him. He finally did land himself a job. He got a job working in a kitchen at a local nursing home. The money wasn't great. But it helped to keep him above water. Plus, it was necessary for him to keep his freedom. One day as he walked to the bus stop.

While he stood there waiting for the bus, at the bus stop. He saw a police car. He thought nothing of it. Until, the police car got close enough for him to see who was driving. All he was able to do, was to shake his head in disbelief. He couldn't believe it was Officer Smith. Officer Smith noticed him too. That's when he stopped the police car. Officer Smith instructed Ty to place his hands on the wall behind the bus-stop. Ty looked at him and said, "Wow!" Officer Smith said, "Wow!", "What?" Officer Smith told Officer Nickel why he stopped Ty. He explains to his partner, that it's always good to check the local street garbage. Then he smiles at Ty, and tells him, welcome back home. He asked Ty, how was his vacation off the streets?

He tells him to stay out trouble, because he had no problems sending back where he just came from. Ty remained there in silence. The Officers got back in their squad car and drove off. Ty got on the bus when it came. Ty continued, on his way to work. At his new job, Ty began to deal with one of his co-workers, that he had already knew. While Dana was working long hours to support the family. Ty was more interested in chasing skirts. He starts one of his many relationships behind Dana's back. At first, he went about his action privately. Then he got to the point of not caring. He began to get lazy with it. It became known. Especially, when he got spotted by a friend of the family. He was at the local supermarket with another woman. Ms. Medina's friend from church saw him. Another time Tanya saw Ty messing with around. She didn't say with who, she just referred to Dana, as Ty's being sneaky. She told Dana she should be conscious of it. She should pay attention more.

Dana and Tanya agreed that many women wanted Ty. Dana took what Tanya said as her being paranoid about the whole situation. After, many allegations about Ty's whereabouts.

Before Dana could confront him about it. Ty did a 360 degree on it. He came clean about it. While Dana worked, Ty played. As he saw that Dana was really fed up with his bull-shit. Fed up to the point that she couldn't take it anymore. With various women calling the house looking for him. Dana told Ty she didn't feel like this was a safe environment for her and the kids anymore.

With him out there doing lord knows what, with lord knows who? Before Dana could ask him to move out. Ty packs up his things and moves out. Word on the streets was he had moved in with a woman, he knew from across town. Somewhere close to where Tanya lived. Tanya would tell Dana, she saw Ty. She would let Dana know who Ty was with. And tell her what he was doing.

She even told her about
the other woman Ty's been
seeing. Most of the time
Dana really didn't care
about who Ty was seeing or
who he was with. she felt
like that was none of her
concern. The truth be
known, Dana was tired of
Ty and his bullshit. Other
times she didn't care that
Tanya let her know,
because her and Tanya was
nosy like that. Also, Dana
would tell Tanya if she saw

her baby father moving like that. It was so weird, that Ty really felt like Tanya was his friend too. To the point, when he saw her, he would acknowledge her presence. No matter who he had with him. Working and taking care of the kids consumed most of Dana's time and life. As time went by, Dana and Tanya friendship grew distant. They still were best friends.

They just didn't have much
free time like they used to
have. They still talked on
the phone, every now and
then. Tanya dealt with a
nice amount of men. One of
things they talked about
was Tanya telling Dana that
she was pregnant. Dana
didn't bother to ask Tanya
who the father was.
She felt like Tanya really
didn't who father was
herself. Dana asks Tanya if
she needed anything.

She told Dana, she was doing just fine. She let it be known, she didn't have any worries or complaints. That's how their last conversation went. When they did talk, the conversations were mainly about each other's kids. And how the kids were doing. Tanya was happy to tell Dana that her God son Markie was about to go away to college. Dana was happy and proud about that.

Ty and his new-found
friends and his new lady
began to make street
moves. Ty was up to his old
tricks again. By now Ty had
been gave up trying to be
the good guy. He felt like,
he got nowhere trying to
be good. Good guy, good
things were not in his blood
stream. Lil Ty was 14
years old, W.B. was 9 and
Myesha was 3 years old.
The boys were, well aware
of who their father was.

They were loyal to their father. Even they were used to Ty and his crazy antics. Dana allowed the boys to visit their father. They were able to spend some time with Ty. What she didn't allow, was when Ty picks up the boys, baby girl was not going with him. She made it clear to him, that she was very protective over, their daughter, her baby. Ty knew not to even go there with Dana.

He actually, agreed with Dana on that one. Much to her surprise, he already knew, she was not playing, when it came down to baby girl.

Chapter 2

Ty was looking for a new scheme. A new come up. Ty wanted to make a big score, once and for all. He wanted something big to get involved with. While in prison, he heard a plan about a bank heist. He wanted in. He wanted a piece of the action. He felt like, he didn't have anything lose. But so much to gain. When he got home from jail. He mainly was laying low.

He knew in a few months. The rest of the crew would be home. Ty's attitude was just like the rest. Nobody wanted to get caught. None of these men wanted to go to the slammer. While in jail, Ty, his cellmate, and his friends from around the way discussed it day in day out, in the prison yard. Ty's cellmate Born came up with a sweet robbery plan. At first, it was so sweet, it sounded too good to be true.

Far-fetched to say the least. After spending so much time, having time in prison. Thinking about the perfect crime to commit. With time to burn, they were able to fine print their plans. The idea which sounded crazy at first. Began to make sense. Now the picture of this heist was beginning to come more and more clearer. So clear, the whole crew saw it. Everyone knew it could be life or death.

Eventually, everyone was release from prison. They began to plot outside of prison. Plans out to be the perfect crime. If they could get away with it? They met up for several weekends. Discussing how it was going to go down. They knew it had to be well executed. If done right, with little to no mistakes being involved. That was the set goal. First, they made sure they scanned the whole bank out.

The whole perimeter inside and outside. They learned where all the outside and inside cameras were located. And where the security guards would be set up at. All the different security guards, schedules were. When would the bank be at its most vulnerable time. They studied when would be the best day and time to do the heist. Many questions had to be answered. Before a move can be made.

Born's cousin Deroid began to date a woman who worked there. He did it mainly to get some inside information. The best way to know how the bank operated, was to know someone who actually works there. While he was dating her, she began to tell him everything they needed to know. Things like what time did the last shift leaves work to go home. When the bank opens for the day.

Also, when it closes for the night. Money delivery days. Days when they had the most security on site. Even the fact, on Wednesdays, while everyone else goes home. One of the clerks stays back. The clerk had to go over the transaction for the week. The clerk also had to close-out some of the accounts of the day. Mainly, he had to make sure all the books were up to date.

He had other various duties also to perform. Which included letting the cleaning service into the bank to clean. After the cleaning crew were finished cleaning. The supervisor of the cleaning service crew would let the clerk know, so he could let them out. The clerk made sure everything was clean and everything was turned off. Then he turns off the remaining lights.

Once he was ready to leave, he put the security alarm on. Once he walked out the bank, the bank had a special shut lock mechanism. Which he couldn't get back inside even if he tried. It was locked from the inside. The bank was locked for the night. What was the best way to get in without being noticed. How to get into the bank undetected.

Sparky and Ty decided to get a job with the cleaning company that cleans the bank. The company that had the cleaning contract with the bank. Ty became the driver of the cleaning company's van. Sparky and Ty were assigned to the cleaning crew, the crew that cleans the bank. For a couple of Wednesdays, they went in with the rest of the cleaning crew. They cleaned the bank like they were hired to do.

While they swept, mop and waxed the floors. They clean the windows and counter-tops. While they were working, they were able to spot and locate all, the security cameras. They knew how it was set up, for themselves. Now, they knew the day and the time. Perfect time because there were little to no action taking place at that time. No traffic on the road. Nobody was hardly on the streets at that time.

No police activity near the bank at that time. With this much needed knowledge. The pieces were all coming together. The following weekend, the men got together, to go over the plan once more. They came with the finalization of what was going to take place. By the time they left their final meeting. Each one knew their position. The roles they must play.

Now, they were just waiting for the day to strike. They all were ready to do this. They knew that Wednesday was going to be the day it was going to go down. They were ready to put their plans into action. They went over the list one last time, on that Monday evening. The night before, after their quick meeting. All the men went on their separate ways. The next day came, Wednesday was here.

The day came to execute the plot that was put into place. The first move they made from the plan, was to stick up the cleaning company vehicle. This was a great move to make. To gain access to the bank undetected. Plus, it made the perfect cover-up. Wednesday evening looked like any ordinary day. Nothing unusual about it. Ty drove out of the cleaning company parking lot.

The five-man cleaning crew were in the company van. They began the trip as usual to the bank. During the drive, the men were holding random conversations as usual. Some listened to the music played in the background. When the van was mid-way towards the bank. When the van stopped at a red light. They were waiting for the light to change. Another van approaches the cleaning company van.

The men in the van next to them had mask on. They ordered them to pull over the cleaning van. At first, Ty didn't want to comply with the demands that was said to him. Once the guys in the moving van saw that the guys in the other van was holding guns. They demanded Ty to pull the van over, and do what the armed man told him to do. That's when Ty did what the masked men told him to do.

They ordered the men to get out of the vehicle. All the men did what they were told to do. Nobody wanted to get hurt. Once they were outside of the work van. They were ordered to strip down. They had to take off their cleaning uniforms. The masked men took their, uniforms and put on the cleaning men's, uniforms. They blind-folded all the cleaning men.

The cleaning men didn't have a clue on what was taking place. They basically didn't know what the hell was going on. The mask men placed the blind-folded men inside the unmarked van. One of the mask men got back into the unmarked van and drove off with the hostages. The two masked who drove the blind-folded workers away, dropped each induvial off in different locations.

That was the orders they receive to make each worker confused about what was going on. That made it difficult to communicate for the workers. So, they couldn't tell who was with them or not. The cleaners understood what was going as far as being in the predicament they were in. Still, they couldn't understand why would somebody want with a cleaning company van?

That was the confusing part about it. Because all they had in the van was cleaning equipment. The question of the day was, who would want to do that? It made no sense to them, what so ever. Let alone, understanding why they were being held against their will. Nobody dared to question anything. They were in fearing for their lives.

Staying alive was more important than anything at this point of time. Nobody wanted to get these men, with these guns mad. The outcome of doing that, would be dangerous. Each man was left alone, by themselves, blinded folded and tied. With no clues of their whereabouts. For all they know, was the fact, that all five of them was in the same predicament.

Nobody saw or knew where they were at. That was the scary part of this ordeal. After plan A, was completed. The remaining men made their way to the bank. Disguised as the cleaning crew. The cleaning van parked in the bank's parking lot. Everything looked and seemed normal. Like any other regular Wednesday evening. They were there undetected. Everything was going as planned.

The cleaning crew began unloading the cleaning van. Bringing out the cleaning equipment. The brooms, mops and other cleaning supplies. They took out the cart that had all the cleaning spray bottles in it. One of the cleaners push the equipment cart. The other men grabbed the mops and brooms and followed behind. The bank clerk opened the bank's doors to let the cleaning crew in.

Once they got inside the bank, the bank clerk told them about the spill in the bank's President's office that needed immediate attention. He was told by his supervisor to tell the cleaning crew to clean that first. One of the crew followed the clerk to the president's office. When he got to the office, the cleaner told the clerk that he got it. The clerk went back to the cleaning crew.

He told them they could get started. He couldn't remember, what was the other task, that he needed the cleaning crew to take care of. He told them, when he remembers, he'll let them know. Before he left the workers alone, he asks them did they need him for anything. They said, "NO!" The clerk went back to do what he was doing. The other 4 began to clean the main level floor of the bank.

The clerk looked at them before he went into the office he was doing work at. The clerk had a lot work that he needed to take care of. The clerk didn't get paid to babysit the cleaning crew. He got paid to do his own job. On the main floor, while they took the ladder to clean unreachable spots. Whenever they came across a camera, they placed black tape over the camera lens.

While another one of the men, the one who was sweeping the floor. He placed the tape over all the reachable cameras. At this point of time, all the men were split up, all around, inside of the bank. They were making sure everything was the way they planned it out to be. They had to be sure before they attempted to make any moves. They knew the security system was not on.

Because the clerk didn't put it on. He would normally put it on after the night was over. They knew just about how everything went from the gathered information they obtained when they did they research of the place. The clerk returned to get one of the workers to clean another spill in his office, that he had just made. To his surprise he walked right into a set trap.

Once one of the assailants pulled out his gun from his work uniform. The clerk was caught up. And it was nothing he could do about it. He ordered the bank clerk to open all the bank safes. He warned the clerk, that if he made one false move, it would be over for him. Because he wouldn't hesitate to kill him. The nervous clerk did what the man ordered him to do.

The clerk did what the men told him to do. The clerk didn't want to lose his life. The men began to fill up big laundry bags full of money. When the bags got to its full capacity. They placed the bags on a long mail cart. Once a mail cart was full. They began to load up another one. All was going as planned. Collecting as much money as possible. One of the men took the clerk to the janitor's closet.

He tied him up as well.
After he opened the last
bank vault. While the
robbery was taking place.
On that cold winter night.
On this quiet street. The
bank stood on a corner of a
block. The bank been there
so long. It was thought and
look upon as a landmark. A
fixture of a community
that didn't have a lot more
to offer. So, it was a
major part in the
neighborhood.

Officer Smith informs his rookie partner Officer Nickels, that he notices something was strange. Something didn't look right to the Officer. What was out of the ordinary to them was one of the bank lights was on, that normally would not be on. The Officers knew on Wednesday at that time of the night, the bank wasn't open to the public. But they also knew, it was the day that the cleaning

company came to clean the bank. They spotted the cleaning company's vehicle. So, they thought nothing of it at first. Officer Smith informed his partner that it wouldn't hurt, if they checked things out. Meanwhile, inside the bank, the bank robbers were already finished up. They already packaged all the bags up. There were ready to make their clean getaway.

So, they thought. When one of the bank robbers looks outside from the bank window. He sees the police car in the parking lot. He saw the police officers standing in front of the police car. Seeing this, the robber immediately informed his partners. Officer Nickels asked officer Smith if he wanted him to call for back up, just in case. Officer Smith became more curious.

After he saw a shadow in the window, where it shouldn't be one at. At that point of time, Officer Smith pulled out his gun. Again, officer Nickels asked officer Smith did he want him to call for back up. Officer Smith informed his partner that they didn't have time to do so. With the criminals seeing the police activities from the window. With that knowledge, the next plan was about to be in effect.

The next part of their great get away. After officer Smith said, what he said. Still, officer Nickels didn't think it was such a smart move, to make. Even though he wasn't sure about, what they were about to get themselves into. Still, he knew he had to back up his partner. Especially since officer Smith was the senior officer of the two of them.

Smith was the officer with the all the experience. The robbers were ready and well prepared for the officers. One of the robbers got the clerk from the janitor's room. He didn't waste any time. He shot the clerk, execution style. With the gunshot to the head. The clerk died right there on the spot. The robbers were prepared to leave with the money and no witnesses behind.

Officer Smith instructed his partner to cover the back door. While officer Smith decided to go through the front door. Little to his knowledge on the other side of the front door the gang of criminals were wanting for him. When Officer Smith opened the door. He walked inside the bank to an ambush. The bank robbers shot officer Smith several times.

With a whole hooray of bullets. Only several actually hit the officer, but the one's that did hit him. Really did hit him good. While officer Smith was being shot up, he was able to get one shot off. The shot struck one of the robbers in the head. Officer Nickels heard the shots coming from the front. He hurries to get to the front side of the building, from the back.

He runs pass the cleaning vehicle, that was parked in the back of the bank. He looks through the bank window, there he saw his partner laying there in a pool of blood. With no movements what so ever. Just there motionless. To make matters even worst. As officer Nickels made his to the door. When he touched the door knob, an explosion went off. The momentum was so powerful.

It knocked officer Nickel a couple of feet away. Luckily, he landed on his behind. Besides a couple of lumps and bruises. Officer Nickels was fine. The bank shortly collapsed, after the fire burned the structure to the ground. Officer Smith's body inside of it. During all the commotion, the assailants was able to get away. They got away with a whole lot of money.

They had come off with a small fortition. They stole over 30 million dollars, with no traces. Everything, including most of the evidence, and officer Smith were burned. It was very hard to find officer Smith's remains. They couldn't locate the clerk's remains either. The cleaning crew workers were released the following day. All were released from different locations.

The police were notified the night, that the cleaning company's van was stolen from an anonymous tip. When the men from the Cleaning company was able to do so, the notified the police what had happened on their ordeals. All of them said, just about the same story. The police were making this a priority, to find out whomever committed this horrific crime. For now, they had no leads, at all.

They finally found the cleaning van. That serve as no help, either. That too was burned beyond recognition, with the remains of a burned human body that was behind the stirring wheel. Whoever would be assigned to this case, will have a hard case to solve. They knew it was the van by its serial numbers. The chief medical examiner told the detectives that they discovered 4 bodies.

In total at the bank robbery site. They were eventually identified by their teeth. As the medical reports came back, the men were identified as Officer John Smith, the bank clerk Thomas Booker, the other body that was found in the bank, one of the bank robbers. His name was Deriod Brown. The body that was found in the cleaning company's van was identified as being David Born Bashman.

With the information the detectives put together. They knew the cleaning company van was stole prior to the actual bank robbery. The detectives knew the other two bodies were part of the robbery. Now the question was, who, what and why? That was the questions, but they had little to no, answers. The case was so difficult, it remained up in the air, for a while.

That sad part about the case was they had two suspects, unfortunately, they both were dead. None of them was talking. After a while of trying to figure something out in this case. The complexity made it an unsolved case for the moment. They told officer Nickels that if he came up with something. They wouldn't mind looking back into it. Then they express their sorrow for his lost.

P.O. Nickels was a little frustrated over them closing the case, so soon. But he respected the fact that they tried. Still, to him, it wasn't good enough. He felt like he at least owed that to his deceased partner. He went through the motion of losing his partner. He felt like losing his partner and nothing was being done about it. That's what, didn't sit right in officer Nickel's stomach.

When Officer Nickels attended officer Smith's funeral, he couldn't help, but feel sad about the whole ordeal. When he looked at Mrs. Smith and their three almost adult children. All he could say at the moment, was that police officer Smith was a great policeman, partner, friend, just a great man and a great person. He let her know that her husband had taught him a lot.

That's when he made up his mind. After the funeral, officer Nickels vowed that one day, he would find, who did this to his partner. He went out on his own time trying to find clues on this case. After all of the hard work he put in. All leads, lead back to Deriod and a guy named David a.k.a. Born. The one thing he learned that Deriod and Born were cousins.

When Nickels visit the neighborhood that surrounded the bank. He went door to door, to see if anyone seen anything unusual or suspicious.
None of them, he spoke to, said they saw anything nor heard anything. All they heard was a loud sound like an explosion. Then it was too late. To response, all they were able to do was to notify the authorities. They didn't know about

anything that happened that night. Officer Nickels wasn't about to give up. He wouldn't quit, until the persons who committed this horrible crime was brought to justice. As the police began to ask people in the neighborhood. Most didn't know what happened. Just about everyone was shocked over the fact. When the detectives told them, what had happened to officer Smith.

That he was murdered during the bank robbery. Some felt bad for the officer who got killed. Other's had a chuckle in their voice. Overall, most didn't care. Most didn't care for officer Smith in the first place. Still, no one could image that someone could be bold enough to do something like that. They couldn't believe, someone had the balls, to pull that crime off.

And kill officer Smith in the process. Pulling off robbing the largest bank in the area. Many was in disbelief. Then top it all off, the criminals around the way was fascinated on what has taken place. That was definitely, the talk of the town. After a bunch of people gave the police department the same attitude of not caring about the case. Among the people in the hood.

Everyone wanted to know did anyone make out with any money, alive. People didn't care who did it, if anyone got away with it, all they knew, they wanted a piece of the pie. The money from the bank, even the F.B.I. wouldn't be able to trace it. The catch was, if anyone got hold of this money, they were good, because the money was still in circulation. Which made it impossible to trace.

That made it the biggest bank heist that anyone ever saw in this part of town ever. It was done so well. Even the federal agents had to admit to that. But the question was, did anyone get away with it? If they did, it took a couple of masterminds to get away, Scott free. A crime that was well executed. Cause they left no type of evidence behind.

The only thing the authorities could do was plan to make sure it didn't happen again. Just in case, if anyone tried to do it again. They made sure they beefed up security. The police department put more officers around all the major local banks. The city officials installed more surveillance cameras, security guards, police officer's presence. No one dared to take any chances with even thinking about robbing a bank. The local officials made sure about that. Nobody was acting out of the ordinary. Most people were in disbelief. No one ever knew anyone who had money like that before. It was like the money upped and disappeared. No money was being spend at all. Ty and Sparky returned work, Monday morning just like the rest of the cleaning crew.

After their crazy ordeal.
All, of the men were told
by management to take the
rest of the week off. The
manager felt bad after
what these men had
experienced. They didn't
have to worry about being
paid for the days off. The
company paid the days,
they were instructed to
take off. The owner of the
cleaning company agreed
with the manager. They
deserve a week off with
pay.

That was the least they could do for them. Everyone knew, that it must have been a traumatizing experience. A life changing event. They even offer to pay for counseling. If any of the men wanted counseling. The men were happy and grateful how management cared about them in that way. Still, the men were shaken up, about what had transpired.

The police detectives came by the job. They wanted to ask some question about how they were carjacked. They wanted to find out who stole the van. They thought maybe they could get some type of leads, from a different perceptive. They were trying to put one and one together. The only thing the cleaning company's workers could say, was they got pulled over and the masked men, told them to get out the van. They were holding them at gun point. After they were taken out the van, the mask men blind-folded them. Then they were ordered to strip, take off their work uniforms. After they were in their underwear, they were placed in another van. The masked men drove them undisclosed sites. They didn't know their whereabout.

When the men finally got released, they were dropped off, by the highway, between highway exits. When they finally took off the prisoner's blindfolds, all the men were able to see, at the time of the drop off point, was the highway. That was about it. When the cops asked them individually, all them said just about the same story.

The men, who were being questioned, by the detectives were just happy that they weren't murdered. The detectives kept on asking them the same question over, and over again. None of the men had any changes in their story. They explained to the detectives that, that's all they knew. When the detectives brought up, what had happened, after the van was stolen, that it was part of a bank robbery, that had taken place. All the men were shocked about that news. They didn't have a clue about that, either. After finding no leads from the cleaning crew workers. Next, they went to investigate the two dead robbery suspects. They found out that one of the suspects had a warrant in Washington D.C...

That suspect's name was Deriod. The warrant was over a case, that had to do with a bank robbery. They're curiosity grew, about this particular suspect. Maybe he was the mastermind of this bank robbery as well. Deriod skipped bail after he was released on bail. The judge issued a bench warrant after he failed to appear on his court date. They immediately knew he was definitely, part of the actual bank robbery. They also found the link between the two dead suspects. They were cousins. Which was yet again, another key factor in this case. They were finding a bunch of key information pertaining to this case. As they dug deeper into each man's backgrounds. Deriod, cousin Dave known as Born just got out of prison. Not long ago. Born had a long rap sheet as well.

He got out after serving time for a bank robbery. Both criminals had lengthy criminal records. Most of all their convictions came from bank robbery. The detectives came up the conclusion that they must of did it. They had to do it themselves, with little to no help. But something was wrong. Something went wrong. They must have told someone their plans.

Because someone wanted these guys to rob the bank. Then they robbed, the bank robbers. All along, little to their knowledge, someone was watching and following these guys. Waited for them to get the money. When Dave got killed by officer Smith. Deriod killed officer Smith. Deriod continued to flee the bank with the money and the van. After he set the explosives off.

He left the bomb behind to blow the bank up, so there will be no evidence left behind. He felt like, even if he left something behind, it wouldn't be traced because it would be blown up, just like the bank. He would be gone before anyone could think about it. Too bad, he didn't get that far with his plans. When he was trying to get rid of the cleaning van.

Which was used to get
inside the bank, and get
away with the money.
When he ditched the van.
He got ambushed. Then
they placed him back in the
van, he was trying to get
rid of. They shot him
dead. Then they placed him
behind the driver's seat.
They took the money. And
put the van on fire with
him in it. That's why they
found Deriod sitting behind
the steering wheel.

The detectives had put that part together with the information they gathered. Still a third party had to be involved. That's who must have gotten away with the money. That was the part that would be nearly impossible to figure out. These guys left nothing behind either. They even made sure they got rid of Deriod in the process. They made sure about that. Yet again, the case took a serious curve after that.

The case became cold after that. They gathered enough evidence on the bank robbery. But they didn't have the slightest clue about, where the money was at? So, they didn't completely solve the case. Just like all unsolved cases, the case went into a box. And was placed in a room in the basement to collect dust. The individuals who got the money, the police didn't have any ideas who they were.

The police had no type of knowledge of them. They planned that caper well. The plans for the ones, who did get away, with the money, was to lay low with the dough. Stay out of site. Pretend like the money never existed. Let time go by. Then after that divide the money equally. Well, that was the plan at first. Of course, it didn't go down like that. First, it started off with five individuals.

Now, it was only three, of them left. All the men made a pact at the beginning. From the start, they all agreed, if any of them were killed under any circumstances. The one or ones who killed, got nothing! They agreed with the terms. But like all plans were made to be broken. Some knew, quite a few wasn't going to make it to the actual payday. One way or another.

That's why they killed Deriod. Set the cleaning van on fire, in the process. The perfect crime. Calls for the perfect getaway. That's why they planned it that way. Before you knew it, three became a crowd. Especially, with one of them, who couldn't be trusted. On top of that, they barely knew the third guy. Born brought him aboard. That guy partner Born got killed during the robbery.

They didn't know the guy at all. They tried to get along with him. But the guy always got nervous around them. They felt like with the pressure, oh boy would crack. Like he could be easily snapped, and easily be broken. They couldn't take the chance, to find out later, what he would do under pressure. So, he had to go. They had to get rid of him. So, it was going to happen. So, it shall be.

The way they got rid of the guy, they paid someone to run over the guy with a car. The car had no papers to it. No license plate, etc. the guy who they paid to do the job, had to wear gloves. So, there will be no finger prints. Once he finished the job, they killed the guy who ran over the other guy. They left the guy in the car, after they killed him. Then they pushed the car into the ocean.

When the detectives found the car, the car turned up on the other side of town. The body in the vehicle was so decomposed, it took them weeks to finally identify who was stranded inside of the vehicle. This crime was done so well. They couldn't place any of this together. The detectives who were looking for this man who was driving the vehicle, that ran the man over.

They looked at it, as a hit and run. But no car ever got linked to the hit and run. They had a hunch, that it was a murder, made-for-hire. They had no evidence to support the theory. Both cases went cold, with no suspects and no clues. Just a clean getaway for the persons responsible. The police department was completely thrown with all these current events.

They got away again, that was the dangerous part of it all. With the third guy out of the picture. Ty and Sparky decided to split the money 40/40. With the other 20% going into drug investments. Ty took his 40% and hid it, very well. Where only he knew, where it was at. He knew, he trusted Sparky. At the same time, he knew, he couldn't trust Sparky. When it came to this kind of money.

No one was to be trusted. Sparky did the same, with just about the same thoughts. That's what made them good crime partners. While everyone else's thoughts were all over the place. Ty and Sparky were way ahead of the game. Ty and Sparky knew how to think, while all this madness was going on. They knew when to get loud and make a scene. Also, they knew when to sit back and observe.

They thought alike.
Normally, you could say, on
the same page. The 20%
was to open, the weed spot
back up. They started
where they left off at.
This time they knew they
weren't going to make the
same mistakes as before.
They were prepared to
make smarter moves. They
bought a candy store. Plus,
the building next door to
the candy store. The store
was there, to be the
cover-up.

They used the old building, next door, as the new drug spot. Quickly, they got a lot of their old customers back. Money started rolling in again. The two men was very smart individuals. They kept their jobs at the cleaning company. At this time, money began to look good again. They were back on top of their game. With so much money to be made.

Chapter 3

Ty remained low-key about everything. He made sure he was far away, as possible from the action. He didn't want to be anywhere near hot street. Plus, he matured a lot, from back then. More focus on the finer things in life. Don't get me wrong. He was still chasing females around. Ty and Dana became cool again, as usual. Somethings will never change.

Things like that. As the
money started to pour in.
Dana became cool enough
to allow him to see the
boys again. Lil Ty and
W.B. were able to spend
the day with their dad.
Sometimes he had the boys
the whole weekend. When
he drops the boys off
home, they walked in with
shopping bags of clothes
and sneakers. Whatever
the boy wanted. They were
able to get whatever their
little hearts desired.

Lil Ty also had an envelope he was instructed, to give to his mother, Dana. The name on the envelope was Myesha. Inside the envelope was filled with money. Ty understood, he wasn't going to see his daughter that often. In fact, he understood, the way he was living, he really didn't want his daughter to be in any parts, of it. He wanted his daughter to be nice and pure. His lifestyle will not be her lifestyle.

He was going to make sure
of that. Dana didn't really
ask or cared about, how Ty
made his money. she was
happy with the fact that
he was taking care of his
kids. His responsibilities.
Just like how he supposed
to. That's all that matters
to her. Nothing was wrong
with, thinking like that
either. The last thing Dana
heard, was Ty had a good
job. He was making good
money on it.

Ms. Medina was worried about Dana's well-being. Which, she always did, and always will be. She always was concerned about her daughters' lives. But, she remained silent throughout the whole ordeal. Ty also, rekindled a relationship with his younger brother, Stuy. He began to help pay Stuy's college tuition. Stuy was 20 years old. He gave, him a job also. He gave him a job at his candy store.

Ty came, to the conclusion, when his father died. Not only did he lose a father, the main man in his life. He realized that Stuy did as well. He could at least give his brother something to build on. He also gave a job to his younger sister, Betty. Her job was to hold the money, deposit the candy store money, with the dirty money, into the candy store's bank, business account. He told her how to do it.

Match every dollar amount with the dirty money, and the candy store money. She had his part of the money from the bank heist. At first, she was holding the money under a brand-new king size bed, he had bought for her. He didn't tell her exactly, where he got the money from. He placed a bunch of crates of money under her King size bed. As many crates that could fit under.

The crates took up the whole length of space under the bed. Then he placed more in her closet. The money remained out of sight, out of mind. He paid her a nice sum for doing that. She was actually, laying down and going to sleep on money. No one in the world would think his 16 years old sister, would have his share of the stolen bank money. Ty had so much money spread out, elsewhere.

He could afford to act like the bank robbery didn't exist. He knew it was limited people, he could really trust. Two people, he knew for sure, that wasn't out to get him was his little brother, and little sister. They were completely loyal to him. When he had the boys on the weekend, he would visit his sister and brother. So, the boys could build a relationship with their aunt and uncle.

Ty's step-mother thought nothing of it. She liked the fact, that he acknowledges his younger brother and sister. And he is spending time with them, with the boys. Which made it all the better, all the sweeter. That's how smart Ty was. He stayed not saying nothing, but yet, all the moves were being made, that nobody would even think he was smart enough, to pull off.

He moved so good, almost impossible to figure out, what's going though, his mind. Ty stayed in an apartment across town. From where Dana and the kids lived. Sometimes one of his lady friends would stay with him. Not lived with him. But she would stay over a couple of days in the week. Because most of the time Ty was busy doing other things, and other women.

He didn't live, too far away from Tanya's place. Sometimes they even ran across one, another. They would see one another at numerous locations. Neighborhood places like the corner bodega, laundromats, supermarkets, etc. They would just wave at one another. They would say "Hi!" and keep it moving. Then it became them having a short conversation.

Then conversations grew longer. She noticed the way he was living. She couldn't help, but to take notice, of the abundance of money Ty had. He wasn't showing off either. It wasn't hard to tell, he had nice things. His car was nice, his watch was expensive. Ty and Tanya were always good friends. Nothing else was ever thought about it. Until, the day Ty saw her, in a certain outfit.

She had on an outfit that were complimenting, all her curves. While they were talking. He couldn't help it. He stirs, at everything else while they held that conversation. She had this look on her face. Her dress was fitting her in all the right places. He kept on complimenting her. He amazed, on how her body has changed, since the last time he saw her. How her body was fitting that dress on her.

She knew he was checking her out. She thought it was cute. She asks him, where he was staying at, nowadays. He told her, where he was staying at, at this point of time. She told him, that he should stop by her place sometime. Nothing less, but to hang-out, a little bit. He said, he wouldn't mind. Then Ty left the store. He thought, not too much about it.

He thought, she'll probably tell Dana, that she saw him. Tanya was like family. They had so much history together. Their lives ran so parallel. When he saw her the next time, he asked about her son, Markie. She told him, he was in college out of state. And he lived on his college campus. When hearing that, Ty immediately dug in his pockets. He took out a whole big roll of money.

He peels off a couple of hundred-dollar bills. He told to give the money to Markie for college. He remained there looking at Tanya's face. Then he told her, he was amazed how time flies. She agreed, "Isn't that the truth!" she said. He replied, "for real!" Before, he left the supermarket where they bumped into each other at. He notices, she was kind of upset.

He asks her, why she was upset? She told him because he didn't come by yet. She told him, she was looking forward to seeing him. He couldn't tell if she was serious or not. He laughed and told her, he didn't want to get her into trouble. Her response was, everyone's grow over here. Then to his surprise, she talks about what kind of trouble could she possibly be getting into.

Then she smiled and walked away. She was sending a whole lot of mixed signals, at Ty. Ty took it as friends, playing around with one another. They knew each other for years. Since Markie didn't have a father, that was active in his life. Ty took Markie under his wing, like a son. Ty treated him like one of his own. His first instinct was maybe, he was over reading everything, that was going on.

He thought maybe she was playing around, she always played around. She was silly like that. Just to see how he would response to it. Everyone, that knows her, knows Tanya was nothing, but a big flirt. You couldn't really, take her too seriously. Of course, neither did Ty. She made him promise, to come by and check out her place. So, he decided to take her up on her offer. He stopped by her place.

He rung her door bell.
Tanya came to the door in
a little see through, house
dress on. The dress was
showing just about
everything. She told him to
have a seat on the couch.
Then she went to the
kitchen to make them some
drinks. She came back to
living room, with drinks in
her hands. She placed Ty's
drink on her glass coffee
table, under a place mat.
She sat on her love seat.

Which was on the side of
the couch. She sat there
with her legs crossed as
sips on her glass of liquid.
He sat there sipping on his
liquid that he brought with
him in a brown paper bag.
She pours in a wine glass
for him. He sat sipping,
shock and amazed at what
he was seeing. The
television was playing low.
The music was playing the
background.

But all focus, was on Tanya's legs. He never looked at her in that shape, form or fashion, prior to that evening. They chilled, had a nice fun conversation. They watched a movie. They talked about old times. After, the movie was over. He began to get ready to leave. He told her, he had to go. He gave her some money. He told her, he had to pick up some more money.

She tells him, he should stop by, more often. He saw she was a little tipsy. Just off the way she was acting. The way she sat there in that little dress, that showed everything, in front of him. But he really did have to pick up some money. They didn't do anything. It was definitely, a different vibe. Another level, in all sorts. Ty left it alone. He kept it moving for the moment.

As, he thought about it. Still, he couldn't figure that out, for the life of him. Anyway, he saw that it was a good spot. Where he could chill at. Whenever he wanted to be away for everyone. He could go to Tanya's place. One night they both was doing a whole lot of drinking. Drinking so much, Ty got drunk. So drunk, he couldn't open up his eyes, or walk.

Because of these circumstances, he couldn't drive home. The way he stood up. He was fighting to stand up. So, he could get up and leave. Every time, he tried to stand up. He had to sit back down. Clearly, he wouldn't be able to make it home, that night. He had no choice. But to ask Tanya, could he crash on her couch for the night. He told her, he'll leave in the morning.

He laid down on her living room couch. As, he laid there, before you knew, he was knocked out, cold on her couch. Tanya, had too much to drink also. She kept on walking pass. In and out of the living room. From her bedroom to the bathroom. From her bedroom to the kitchen. Every time she makes her moves, she stares at Ty sleeping on her couch.

She had a tee-shirt on with no panties on, under, at this point of time. Ty was fully clothed. The only thing Ty took off was his footwear. Tanya went back to her bedroom. She got back into her bed. Close her eyes for a bit. A short while later, she went to the bathroom. Then she went to the kitchen to get a glass of water. She walked through the living room.

She was looking, watching Ty as he slept. Ty was there suspended in time. She walks through the living room, yet again. She walked up to the couch, where Ty laid at. He had his legs wide opened not conscious of his surroundings. Thoughts began to run through Tanya's head. Thoughts she wanted to act on. She caught a visual of what she wanted to transpire.

Just the thoughts of it, had her licking her lips. All along, Ty remained there, sleep, knocked out for the count. Tanya sat on Ty's lap. She began to grind, a little on him. He made movements. She began to unbutton his shirt. She started rubbing his chest. She began to feel on his pants. Rubbing his legs. He woke up, when she went to kiss him on his lips. Ty began to kiss her back.

Still, he was a little unconscious. He held her with pressure. He began to feel on her too. One thing lead to another, they began to kiss more passionately. Things got more and more intense. An unstoppable energy that had to be address. Tanya woke up on Ty's chest, the next morning. Then she kisses his chest and rubbed it. Ty woke up, he pulled her head up to where he was at.

He began to kiss her, as he caresses, her bottom. They turned over and started doing it, all over again, again and again. They went at it, the whole entire weekend. He winds up staying there the whole weekend. They agreed, this would be, they own little hidden secret. Both, of them didn't want Dana to find out this. Neither one of them, wanted to stop either. It went beyond a one-night stand.

They wanted to feel this vibe, for a little while longer. So, they began a sexual friendship. A friendship with no strings attached to it. Just a mutual understanding, it would be sex, nothing more, nothing less. Just a whole lot of it. When the time called for it. Some path must be crossed. When the roads meet at a crossroad. Tolls must be paid. In life, it is, what it is.

That's just the way it goes. Ty decided to hang out with his boys for a night. Friday night was a perfect day to do so. Which he normally didn't do. But this time, he wanted to get out and about. See how the world was. What was popping out there, on the streets. He wanted to paint the town. See how the world has changed. Since he's been home from prison, he hasn't gone out that much.

From when he came home, he was playing it low-key. Ty got bigger in size, his hair wasn't growing like it use too. Things were clearly not like how it once was. He went to a bar with a couple of his boys. He dresses up with a nice amount of jewelry. Things he usually wouldn't wear. They park outside of the bar. They got out the car, cracking a bunch of jokes, having fun.

They went inside, ordered a couple of drinks. After the drinks, they decided to go to the back of the bar, where the pool tables were at. After playing a couple of rounds of pool. Another group of guys came to the back of the bar, where the pool tables were at. Also, where Ty and his friends were at. They noticed the crew of guys were all drunk. Plus, they were there looking for trouble.

They kept on starting trouble with a variety amount of people. They kept on asking people, what they were looking at. Ty and his friends tried to ignore the temptation of drama. That was being served from all different angles in the pool hall, they were in. Even when the fight initially broke out between the group of the drunk guys and other group of guys.

The men began to fight all over the pool hall. When Ty and his friends were trying to leave, they got caught up in the brawl. When one of Ty's friend got sucker punched. They had no choice, but to defend themselves. They had to fight like everyone else in this bar fight. While Ty was fighting one induvial. The guy Ty were fighting friend pulled out a gun. He began to aim it, in Ty's direction.

He was planning to shoot Ty. Ty's friend reached in his waistband. He pulls out his gun. Quickly he pulls the trigger on his gun. He shot the guy, just in time, before he could shoot Ty. Ty's friend shot the guy in the legs. When the guy got shot, he dropped to the ground, dropping his fire arm. While the fighting was still going on. The lady who were serving the drinks ran to the front to call the police.

Ty retrieves the gun, when it hit the ground. When the cops came on the scene. The cops came to the bar to stop, the big bar fight. Ty and his friends were surprised to find out, who the guy was, who was trying to shoot Ty, the guy was actually the owner of the bar. The reason, why he was trying to shoot Ty, was because Ty was fighting with his brother.

33333

33333333

last time, that was everyone's last warning. All fingers pointed in Ty and his friends' direction. When they searched them, they found a weapon that was fired, on Ty's friend's waistband. They arrested him. When they searched Ty, Ty still had the gun of the bar owner, in his pocket. The one that fell to the ground. The one he picked up from the floor, when the guy dropped it.

Ty retrieves the gun, when it hit the ground. When the cops came on the scene. The cops came to the bar to stop, the big bar fight. Ty and his friends were surprised to find out, who the guy was, who was trying to shoot Ty, the guy was actually the owner of the bar. The reason, why he was trying to shoot Ty, was because Ty was fighting with his brother.

The gun, the bar owner pulled out, was registered to the him. He had a legal fire arm. The whole story got turned around with the quickness. Especially, when the cops announced, that if they didn't find who were shooting in the bar. They were going to lock everyone up, who was in the bar. When they said that! Just about everyone in the bar had some dirt on them.

The cops let it be known,
that everyone was going
down. Plus, the bar and
pool hall would be closed
for good. As the cops
began to search everyone,
one by one. People began to
point fingers at Ty and his
friends. The cops decided
to check Ty and his friends
first. They had nowhere to
go or hide. The whole bar
was flooded with police
officers. When they asked
everyone in the bar for the

last time, that was everyone's last warning. All fingers pointed in Ty and his friends' direction. When they searched them, they found a weapon that was fired, on Ty's friend's waistband. They arrested him. When they searched Ty, Ty still had the gun of the bar owner, in his pocket. The one that fell to the ground. The one he picked up from the floor, when the guy dropped it.

The one that was going to be used, to shoot him. Ty got arrested also. He tried to explain, why he had the guy's gun in his pocket. But, they didn't want to hear any explanations at that point of time. when they got to the precinct, what they thought was self-defense, became everything else, but self-defense. They were changed with a hooray of charges.

You name it, they were being charged with it. All the way from them sticking up the bar, starting the bar fight to stealing the bar owner's firearm. With the charges mounting up. Ty was looking at least 20 years in prison. So, the district attorney offer Ty a plea of 10 years. He was advised to take by his paid lawyer. At first Ty wasn't interested in taking a plea deal. Ty was 35 years old at the time.

To him, it became simple
mathematics. As, he sat
and thought about it, in his
jail cell, on Riker's Island.
It didn't take a rocket
scientist, to figure this one
out. In 20 years, he'll be
55. In 10 years, he'll be
45. The simple move would
be, to take the 10. His
lawyer also told him, if he
blows trail it was a
possibility, he could get
more than 20 years. At
least, he wouldn't be that
old when he gets out.

With a twist of events. Placed him back behind bars. Ty had no words to say on it. He had to deal with his reality, he was back in the joint. He was here for years to come, that's all he knew. He felt like it was all a big set up. But he couldn't put his finger on it. Maybe it was karma catching up to him. Some way, somehow, he winds up behind bars again. He knew one thing for sure, he knew the bank heist money would be waiting for him, when he gets home from prison. With no heat, what so ever. It would be money, good money. What a perfect way to lay low, prison, right up under their noises. When Ty called Dana from jail. He told her what happened. He really didn't know, if she believed him or not. He just was letting her know where he'll be staying for the next decade at. He told Dana to tell their daughter that he was dead. He also mentions to Dana, to tell the boys not tell Myesha that he's alive. He really didn't even know if Dana ever spoke about him to their daughter. Realistically, he couldn't control anything that happens outside, while he's there inside. When it came down to things, like that.

He let Dana know, that he was sending his little sister to give her some money. He explains to her that he had a little stash of cash, in his place. Dana went on to say, she didn't want any of his dirty money. Ty replied with, "Yeah," "Ok!" he still insisted that his sister was going bring her the money anyway. Before she could say anything else, he hung up the phone. She was mad for the moment.

She really wanted to tell him, what he could do with his money. Once, she calmed down, she was alright with it. What angered her the most, was the fact, that Ty turned out to be a big disappointment, in her life. After thinking about what she said, she quickly took that back. He was the co-creator of her most precious, valuable assets, which were her children.

The loves of her life. Later, that week, Ty's sister, Betty dropped off the money to Dana like Ty said, she would. Betty came by Dana's apartment. Betty was the only person, who had a key to his apartment? While Betty plans were to drop off the money and keep it moving. But when she saw her niece and nephews, she stayed for a little while. She already knew Lil Ty and

W.B. from when Ty used Come by with the kids. Ty used to visit his step-mother with the kids. She was thrilled to see Myesha. She began to play with the young toddler. Dana saw how the two of them, took a liking to one another. When Betty asks Dana could she take the kids out with her sometimes. She told her that it would be okay for her to do so.

She tells Betty, she could take Myesha by to see her mother. Also, she could take Myesha places, when she took the boys. Dana didn't have a problem with Betty taking the kids out. She felt like it would positive for her to have some type of relationship with their father side of the family. The main person Ty kept in contact with, was his little sister.

He told her as well, not to bring him up to Myesha. If the question does come up. She was told also, to tell her, he was dead. She didn't understand what he meant by that. When he explained it to her? She understood where he was coming from with that. After Ty spend a couple of years in prison. Tanya came to visit Ty in prison. She came many times afterwards.

She was the one who was actually there for him. She didn't let anyone know what she was doing. Or, where she was going. She always left money for his commissary. After the visit was over. He was grateful that she came. For anyone to care about him at his present state in his life, spoke volumes. The first 5 years were hard for him. After knowing, the realization kicked in.

He wasn't going anywhere no time soon. The conclusion of that was, it is, what it is. He knew he'll be back sooner than later. One day he'll be able to leave this joint. His mentality was, shit at least he wasn't in the can for life. That was the main concern. Ty had to sit in prison, while the world goes around and around. Ty's little brother stayed managing the candy store.

Sparky continued to run
the drug spots. Sparky
gave Ty's little brother a
cut of the spot money. Not
the same percentage he
would of gave Ty. But
some, a small percentage.
Sparky liked the way Stuy
was carrying himself. Not
because he was a hoodlum,
or a rough and tough guy.
He saw and liked the fact,
that Stuy was comfortable
in his own skin. He saw
that Stuy really loved the
candy store.

He likes his attitude about it, so much. Sparky decides to give Stuy a proposition, that he couldn't refuse. He offers the ownership of whole the candy store to Stuy, for little to nothing. Stuy was happy with the opportunity that was given to him. He works off the amount, he needs to make to purchase the candy store. The candy store became known as, Stuy's candy Shop.

His store with no strings attached. Stuy's mother was so happy and proud of him. The only thing Sparky wanted all along. He got. He wanted the drug spot with no connections. That's really what Sparky wanted out of the deal. He felt like, he didn't owe Ty anything after that.

After a year with the spot Sparky decided to close up shop. He wanted out of the drug game for good.

Sparky left town with his wife and kids. He took his money from the bank heist and left. Never to be seen or heard from, ever again. Beside all the drama with Ty and all the madness that came along with it. Dana finally got the message, she was going to have to do this alone, with raising her children. With this new episode of Ty's life, she wasn't trying to be a part of it anymore.

She got fed up with the nonsense, for good. She grew tired of it. Ty and his games, with him not taking life seriously. By the time Myesha became 7 years old. Dana had to make a life decision. That will affect the rest of her life. She knew the choice had to be made. The choice of really leaving the love of her life, the father of her children, for once and all. Dana believed in giving a Blackman a chance.

She also knew, she couldn't keep on living life like this way, any longer. It was time to move on, she just had to. No one could function being suspended in time. While Dana worked. Ms. Medina spent a lot of time with Myesha. That was the daily activities for Ms. Medina and Myesha. Granddaughter and grandmother. Ms. Medina took Myesha all over the place. Places of interest, places that educate.

She loves the fact, that her little grandbaby girl was growing into such a beautiful, smart little girl. Myesha always was interested in learning something, she never learned before. Myesha always enjoyed time with her grandmother. She founded her grandmother to be very interesting. Also, a bunch of fun when the two of them got together.

They created a very special bond between the two of them. Besides Dana, her mommy, her grandmother, Ms. Medina, was one of the most important people in her young life. As Myesha got old enough to begin to know what was going on. Myesha was always questioning everything. That's how she was. She was always looking to learn.

Always wanting to know,
what things was, and how
things operate. Ty was
always involved in Myesha's
life. Even if, it was by far.
Many times, he was there.
She just didn't know it.
Like her christening
service, he sat at the back
of the church. Out of
sight, out of mine.
Ty loves his daughter,
more than he loves himself.
His one and only baby girl,
his beloved daughter.

Who he loves with all of his heart. He wanted to stay far away as possible, from her. And yet, he wanted to be close to her. He wanted to keep her pure as possible. He remained invisible to her. Many occasions, he was present for her. Before he came across bad times. Before he got incarcerated. Myesha memory of him, did not exist.

As time went by, Dana's youngest sister Dameeka went from being a little girl, to now being a grown woman. After she finished college, she began dating a guy named Dean. Dean was a neighborhood guy from around the way. He lived a couple of blocks away. Most of her family didn't know or heard of this guy before. Word on the streets was, he lived in the new buildings in the neighborhood that was built several years ago. That's the reason why many of the friends and family didn't know him. Some never saw him before. Dean was an up and, in coming force, to be reckoned with. Though they didn't know him personally, they heard about him. Most people in the neighborhood knew he wasn't a punk. Not a weak individual.

Most of Dameeka's family warned her not to mess around with this guy. They told her not to do it. Just like any other naïve young lady. Who thinks she knows it all. Thinks she has everything mapped out. Thinks she has it all together. Thinking she's in control. Who felt like she's grown. Grown enough to make her own choices and decisions. On, what matter's in her own life.

When it was all said and done. Dameeka followed her heart. Not anyone's opinion of him. She dated him for a while. Ms. Medina knew all too well, about that. Ms. Medina knew how to support her daughters, no matter what. She respects her daughters and their own choices, in their lives. Even if she doesn't agree with them. Ms. Medina learned to let things in life, flow.

After a year of dating.
Dean and Demeeka had a
daughter, together. A
couple of months later, she
moved out of her mother's
place. She moved in with
Dean. Dean was known as a
lower level hustler from
around the way. Whenever,
he came around. He always
seems to have an attitude.
He was the type of dude to
question his lady's
whereabouts all the time.
Questions like who, what,
why or when and how?

Things like what she was wearing. Where and who was going to see her in the places, she was going to. He was an extremely possessive person. Word on the street was, Dean was being verbal and physical abusive to Dameeka. Whenever someone questioned her about it, she always got defensive. Defending her man's ways and actions.

Her excuses were, it was rumors, just rumors. That was her excuse to her family. Dameeka never showed any signs of being abused, in any kind of way. She did remain out of sight all the time. So, it was easy to stay out of mind. No one knew anything that was going on, in her life. Dealing with Dean, she became distant. When Dameeka came to family functions.

She starts off, happy and talkative. When he comes around, she becomes quiet a secretive. When he's around her, her whole mood and demeaner changes. Also, she becomes nervous. Still she pretended like it was all good and everything. So, well, no one was able to put a finger on it. Whenever, he came late to a family function, that was a sign that he only came to pick her up.

After she makes him a plate to go. They quickly left. Nobody, even gets a chance to hold a conversation with Dean. He stayed very territorial. When it came down his and Dameeka's relationship. Even when she was on the phone with her mother and sisters. They could tell when Dean was in the same room as her. Dean was something else with his. I guess, you can call it obsession.

Dameeka remains secretive about her and Dean's business, as if nothing was going on. Because of Dean she wasn't able to watch Myesha for Dana, like she used too. To make matters even worst. When Myesha turned 7, Dana came across, some bad luck of her own. The old man doctor, she was working for health stayed fading. What they thought, took a turn for the worst.

After a few days in
intensive care, Dr.
Silverman succumbed to his
heart condition. He died
later, that same week. It
came as a shock, to
everyone in the client. No
one was excepting this.
It came like a ton of
bricks, for people like
Dana, his workers. It
became an unplanned turn
of events, that has taken
place. It seemed like it
came out of nowhere.

Dana found herself right back where she started from. A mother of three, no job and no man to step up and help her take care of it all. Rock bottom has finally caught up to Dana. She couldn't help but be depressed about it all, the whole ordeal. After months of being unemployed. The unemployment checks ran out. Dana was out there faithfully looking for employment for the whole duration of the time.

She went on many interviews, somedays more than one. She didn't let pride stand in her way either. She was ready, willing and able to do anything to feed her family and put a roof over their heads. Most of the jobs she tried to get, didn't fit her schedule. Before she had a bunch of people, willing to help her out, chip in. To help by watching her kids while she works.

Nowadays, everyone was older, they had families of their own now. They had to worry about, looking out, and take care of their own families. Plus, Dana knew Ms. Medina was getting older and older. Dana didn't want to put her burdens on her mother. With all her responsibilities, that she crated herself. Ms. Medina was rapidly reaching her senior years.

Beyond popular belief. Ms. Medina wasn't a young lady anymore. She couldn't get around like she uses too. Nobody said she was an extremely old lady. But she did have nice age on her. She was a grandmother. Gracefully, looking nice in her silver fox years of existence. All her children, including Dana wanted her to relax. She was already retired. They wanted their mother to enjoy life.

Raising kids, she has already done that. She has been worrying, taking care of everyone else for years. It's about time for her to enjoy her own life. Time for herself. Which she well deserved. For Dana, money became hard to save. Let alone to come by. Especially, when there's no money coming in. Not only was the cost of living was raising. Rent went up as well.

And one thing was for
sure, when it's time to pay
rent. Rent waits for no
one. After a while of
trying to hustle to get the
rent. She had to seek
shelter for her and her
kids. After losing her
apartment. Which she had
for way over a decade.
Her mother's apartment
didn't have enough room for
her and the kids. Really,
she didn't want to do it.
She had no choice.

Her back was against the wall. She had to go into the shelter system. Without a job, she couldn't afford a babysitter. So, working became even harder to find. She needed help. Dana knew not to let her pride get in the way. While in the shelter, she was able to seek other government programs. Her faith in God, kept her afloat.

Knowing about his mercy and grace kept her going. She always believed in God. Deep in her heart. She always felt like, God's got this. He never let her down before. So, why would he let her down now. At this point of time, she stayed mainly to herself. She knew, she had to go through this alone. She took this time to focus on herself. Dana found time to reinvent and redefined herself.

With that time, she became a better person, a stronger one too. Learning herself, finding her inner strength. Gaining strength not only for herself, but for kids also. Many men came on to Dana. Many men promised, her the world. All types of different approaches, still the same outcomes. Men came from all different directions. Different types of men in life.

Dana was a very attractive woman. Men loved the way she carried herself. The way she looked, moved and acted. Her beauty was beyond skin deep. Her inner-glow was to die for. Her curvy precious body frame. When she walks in room full of men. All eyes would be on her. As she walked down the street, men stopped what they were doing. Cars drove slower, when she was in the driver's view.

Some was amazed by the way she walked. She didn't have to wear, any revealing clothes, or very sexy outfits. She could have on sweat pants and a tee shirt. She still got full attention. When she opens up, her mouth, forget about it. Her intelligence made her a total package, a perfect catch, worth catching. A strong black woman with brains and beauty. Everyman's dream woman.

Every King would love to have her as their Queen. Even other women had to give it to her, acknowledgement. All the ladies had to respect. On top of that, the way she treated and took care of her children. Superwoman, super human being. Laws of gravity defines her as being a Goddess. All levels of attraction. She had it all. Most felt that about her, except her.

They thought the world about her, even if it was unwanted. But with her reality of her own life. How they felt wasn't the way, she felt. She really didn't feel pretty at the time. Her beauty wasn't that important to her. It wasn't that she didn't care about herself. She kept up with her hygiene, made sure her and her kids had clean clothes to wear. She always tried to look on

the bright side of things.
Even in the time of
darkness. Still, her
approached, acceptance of
people, and things, she
always remained there with
an open heart. When she
was sad, you couldn't tell.
Because she always had
smile on her face. That,
out shined the hurt inside.
Being pretty for someone
else's acceptance, that was
the last thing on her mind.

Her main, focus was the survival of herself and her children. Her children came first. She really had no time to look, let alone deal with a man. Just to be dealing with one. Dana was the type of person, when she's with someone, she gives a 100%, in a relationship. Since, she didn't have a 100% to give. So, she chose not to deal with anyone. She had her own issues to deal with.

Being in a relationship was not a priority to her. She was finally getting Ty completely out of her system. That long termed relationship with Ty, took a lot out of her. She found closure within her mind, body and soul. Relationships, she just didn't want to be in one. While she was in the shelter system, she was issued a case worker.

She went to meet her case worker, for the very first time. Her case worker's name was Mr. Jonathan Gilmore. The first time they met was when Dana needed some papers filled out for Myesha's school. Mr. Gilmore went on to say he heard so much about her. Dana looks at him with a puzzled expression on her face. She wonders what could he have possibly heard about her.

He told her why he said, what he said. The things he was hearing about was only good things. Once he explained, himself more. Her facial expression and attitude changed, for the better. He liked the little things that she did. The little things that don't get recognized. He especially, like the fact that she's always helping people, who needed help. She spent time talking, listening to people, who overwise, wouldn't have been heard. He admitted that he liked that quality in her. What amazed him the most was, even though she was going through her own reasons why she was in this family shelter. She still had time and a heart to help people. He always said, she had special qualities, that was hard to find nowadays. At that time, Mr. Gilmore gave her many ways and resources to help her to get back on her feet. She thanked him. For all the information he has provided her with. Mr. Gilmore saw the fact, that Dana didn't really belong there at the family shelter. Dana just needed a chance. She was there because of circumstances. He could tell by her character. He saw the desire in her eyes. The drive, the will in herself, to find, to make a better way for herself and her children. Mr. Gilmore couldn't help but to respect and admire that about her. Mr. Gilmore made it his personal business to make sure she got back on her feet. He witnessed the determination she possessed. Not like any other case he had prior too. Her ambition was serious and real, about being somebody in life, some day.

You had to honor and respect that in a person. Meanwhile, Dana distanced herself from her family and friends. Because what she was going through made her become distant, secretive person towards her love ones. She rather, keep the bad or good news to herself. All she had left was her pride and her spirit. She wasn't about to let someone take that away from her.

Also, she didn't want any pity parties over her current situation. She didn't want anyone looking down at her. Like she was a failure or something. She understood and accepted where she went wrong at. Also, life can take some weird turns in it. you could have everything your heart desires one day. The next day you could wake up and have nothing. What can't break you, only can make you stronger.

Dana knew she had hit rock
bottom. It was only one
way to go. And that would
be up. Most importantly,
she wanted to go up the
right way this time. It
lasts longer to do so, in
the long run. Not only did
she believe in this. She
also, lived this way. That's
the main thing, pay
attention to what's going
on, at all, times. Positive
thoughts, way and actions
brings fourth positive
outlooks.

Which in return becomes positive results. She remembered her mother using that saying, throughout her childhood. Her mother said it so much, when she thought about it, she got a visual of her mother actually, saying it. Whenever she sat and reminisced about that quote, all she could do was smile and look at the floor and shake her head.

One thing that was sure,
that saying was all so true!

Chapter 5

Jerome Bridge was born in Brooklyn, New York. He grew up down south. He was offered a job, in New York city, as police officer. The job was offered to him after he retired from the U.S. army. The first thing he did before he took the job, New York. He took his wife and kids on nice long vacation. After his vacation was over, before he left the south, he paid his grandparents a visit.

He told them what was on the horizons, for him and his life. What was his next plans. The next move, he was going to make. He let them know, he was leaving the south. And he was moving back up north. Back to New York, his birth place. He spent quality time with the people, who raised him, his grandparents. They gave him their blessing.

Later, he finishes packing his belongings. Him, his wife and kids got into his car. Then they headed north. They went towards their new destination, New York city. The big apple. His wife and kids were so happy to get to go to New York city. They had a hooray of questions to asked him about New York. Jerome wife and kids never lived in New York, before. They all heard so many stories about it, though.

Questions like, how does it feel like, to live in New York city? See, his wife and kids were raised in the south. So, this experience was new to them. They had so many questions, that they needed to be answered. As, they ask, Rome had an answer. He explained to his kids, he didn't really remember too much about N.Y.C. Not even, how it felt to live there.

To him, New York was all
but a distant memory.
What he did remember, he
had to be honest about it.
Because it was a painful
memory. The painful
memory of his mother's
death. That was the most
hurtful, painful feeling, he
had ever experienced, in
his life. The saddest part
as well. After his mother's
death, family life for him,
would never be the same.

His father couldn't raise him and all his siblings by himself. What he thought was going to be temporary. The notion of, one day, sooner or later, his did would come for him. Which never happened. He was forced to stay down south, and live with his grandparents. His grandparents wind up raising him. To him, not only did he lose his mother. He also, felt like he lost his father, as well.

His father did sent money down south. To help to raise him financially. To take care of him. As, a kid, he wasn't thinking about it in that manner. So, after going through the motions, of not feeling wanted. Thanks to God, he had strong grandparents, who were there for him. Who kept him going. Whenever he was down on himself, they were there, to pick up him back up.

To help lift his spirits up. Let him know, that his family do care and love him. His childhood was complicated. Hectic, to say the least. Truthfully, he didn't sign up for any of that. With all the things, he was dealt with. That's when he decided to try. That was the least thing he could do. That's when his life changed. He went from misery to triumph.

He wanted to be the best person, he could possibly be. He realized, he had nothing to lose. Yet, he had so much to gain. The courage to still get up. The courage to be somebody. To make something out of yourself. He could have allowed all the cards he was dealt, dictate is his life's outcome. Instead, he took all the negative feelings and energy, he had bottled up inside.

He turned all of that around. He made it into a positive. Positive light, that shined throughout his body. A burning light that kept on shining. Coming out of a dark tunnel. A dark place in life. Light, he created to give himself, life beyond the pain. Once, he did that, he suffered no more. That's what made him, the man his was. He told his kids. He made himself a foundation.

The foundation of his life was based on living a good productive life. He became the rock of this foundation. The root of this structure, is the making of a strong family. A family built on values. A family, him and his wife created. Which became a powerful bond between man and woman. That was the support beams of the family structure. The family, the root of love.

Family love will always remain priceless. Makes, no mistakes about it, either. He was happy to go to the state, where it all began for him. The borough, he came from. Jerome was looking forward to what life had in store for him. They went to the house they purchased in Queens. Not too far, not too close, either. A nice little distance from the precinct he'll be working out of.

Jerome was happy and excited beyond belief. To be returning home, and to try to make a difference, in the community he was born in. He ready to get started, he was ready for his new mission in life. First, he had to finish settling in. Him and wife went to visit several churches around where they lived at. Some were local, others were a further distance from their house.

They both liked the one they had visited in Brooklyn. After going a couple of Sundays, they became members. Everything was starting to come together for them. Which was great. Mrs. Bridge went to the local public schools. She registered the kids in their proper schools, for their proper grades. After that was completed. Making all the necessary adjustments, in their new area.

The transition has taken place. Mrs. Bridge was able to get a job at the local veteran's hospital. She was able to get the job with no problems. She was a very highly experienced registered nurse. She became a nurse overseas. While she served in the military herself. She was a veteran herself. She worked out of many veteran's hospitals all over the world.

One thing for sure. They had to get used to, not living an army lifestyle. Now, they must learn to live like civilians, all over again. In the army, that's where they met at. That's where they fell in love at. And they've been together, ever since. During the time, they gave birth to two wonderful kids. That they absolutely adored. They were good people. They had such a great family.

Chapter 6

As, everything began to come in place. The programs that were offered and provided at the shelter for Dana. Dana was able to learns a new trait. She went back college to finish up her education. After getting her college degree. She was able to find a good paying stable job. Not only a job. She was able to find a career. She was able to get a place of her own again.

She moved into a low-income based apartment, in a nice building complex. She received after school care, for Myesha. All the government assistance that was entitled to her, she took. Rightfully so, she should have had. Lil Ty saw his mother's struggles first hand. Also, he witnessed, her triumph over all the diversity, she had to go through. He loved that about her.

She didn't quit, she kept on fighting. What they experienced, made him even more closer to his mother. Make no mistakes about it, her kids weren't happy about, what had taken place. They knew their mother, who was a strong, caring, loving woman. Who only cared about what was best for them. They relied on her. She was everything to them.

As she begins her new journey in life. She finally opens back up to her family and friends. The truth, her truth came out. What has been going on in her life. What she endured. She thought, her family would look at her differently. But they didn't. they loved her unconditionally. They were in full support of her. Happy to see her again. Most of her family couldn't comprehend with the fact on why she didn't reach out to them for assistance. Why she didn't ask for any help. She told them, she had to do this one alone. What she went through made her a stronger person. Clearly, it made her a better woman. An independent woman. Who could stand on her own two feet. She didn't need to depend on anyone. She could maintain on her own. Now, she could raise her children on her own.

She didn't need anyone's help. When it came to this aspect of life. Everyone in her life found a new level of respect for her. Which was a great thing for Dana. She was back with her family. Just like she supposed and needed to be. Family, was the most important thing in one's life. Every now and then, Mr. Gilmore would come by to check up on Dana. He came by on his off time, to do so.

It wasn't hard to tell that he really liked Dana beyond being her case worker. Even her kids noticed it. Her kids respected Mr. Gilmore. Dana didn't view him, in that shape form and fashion. She wasn't into him like that. Deep down inside, she knew this was crazy and all. As crazy as it sounds, Dana still had feelings for her baby's daddy. She did had to admit, to one of her friends, that Mr. Gilmore

was fine. When she did
speak about Mr. Gilmore,
she always came out
complementing him so many
ways. All the good things
were said about that man.
Saying to everyone, who
ask? How handsome, tall,
overall how just a great
caring, loving person he
was. She feels like, he was
special. In a class, by
himself. How she felt, she
didn't want to lead anyone
on, especially, a person who
she cared and admired.

She knew Mr. Gilmore was a good, grown man. As she always stated before, where her feeling was still. Clearly, she knew things could never be the same between them. She understood, there's no such thing, as turning the hands of a clock backwards. She told Mr. Gilmore how she felt, at the present time. she also, mentioned that she valued his friendship greatly. She went on to

say, she really cared about
him. She told him, if he
really cared about her.
Which he did. He'll be
willing to wait for her. For,
she truly appreciated their
friendship. Mr. Gilmore
looked directly into her
eye. He reassured her,
that he'll be there for her.
"As, long as takes" came
out his mouth afterwards.
Also, as long as, she
wanted him to be. Nobody
needed to know, only the

two of them knew truly what the extent of their friendship was. The level of their friendship, relationship. The main focus, was about the two of them. They only knew what it consisted of. Put it like this, whenever she needed or wanted him, on all levels. All of that, was taken care of. During the process of her getting back on her feet. And staying there.

Every once in a while, she would give Tanya a call. Her best friend, to see what was going on in her life. She tells her about the passing of her old boss. The reason why she lost her apartment. How she fell on hard times. How she was able to get back on her feet, and now how she was stronger than ever before. She let her know, she had a new apartment. After she went through the shelter system.

Not only did she get a new
apartment, she also got a
new job and career. She
also mentions her new guy
friend. Tanya was overly
interested in knowing about
that. She was interested in
what Dana was talking
about. As she begins, to
break it all down to Tanya.
She explained the reasons
for her actions. How she
went homeless due to the
fact of being unemployed.
She talks about living in

the shelter with her kids. Like she tells Tanya all of that was done. She went through it. And now she was in a way better position, than she ever was in before. She met a nice man during the process. She stated that, her friendship with her new guy wasn't that serious. Not because of him. She explains, she was the one that wasn't ready for anything serious.

Over all, her guy friend was a kind, sweet, caring and loving man. she even tells Tanya about her and her guy friend having several sexual encounters. During the time they were together. She let Tanya know, she wasn't ready. Even though things went down. But still she wasn't ready. If he was to ask her to marry him. She would say, Yes! Because she knew it was hard to find a man like that.

A person who genuinely cares about a person. People like that are very valuable which makes them priceless. Dana knew for sure that he cared about her. It was no need to even question that. Because she knew the answer for sure. She poured out her heart and feelings to her trusted friend Tanya. Tanya remained there silent on the phone. Just absorbing the information as Dana provided it.

Tanya went on to ask her, how did the kids feel about that? Dana told her that the kids respected and adored him. Tanya was on the other phone receiver completely surprised, with what she was hearing. Tanya had her mouth wide opened with what she was hearing. She really wasn't expecting that. Tanya couldn't help but to ask her about Ty. Dana reply was "What about?" she told

Tanya that Ty was her past. Tanya response was, "Oh really!" "I hear that, girl." came shortly after. Then Tanya asked Dana the million-dollar question, that she was dying to ask her. She asks her did Ty know about that? Also, how would he feel about? Dana responded abruptly to answer Tanya's question, with a no. And why should she care. Tanya continued her questions, by asking

Her, when was the last time she actually heard from Ty. Dana didn't hear from Ty in many years. After she fell on hard times, they had lost contact with one another. Tanya went on to say Why? She told Tanya she didn't have a phone nor an address. So, keeping in contact was completely impossible. She also didn't know what prison Ty was in. To even know where he was at.

Tanya wanted to know, did
Dana live with her new guy
friend. She tells Tanya,
No. They weren't that
serious. She wasn't serious
about anything like that at
the present time. what she
wanted to do was take
small steps, when it came
down to getting into real,
serious relationship. Dana
did have to admit, to
Tanya that she still has
love for Ty. She just
wasn't in love Ty anymore.

Like she had already stated, that was in her past. Tanya made sure she heard everything Dana said. She hears it all, loud and clear. Tanya asked Dana how was she going to get in contact with Ty, sooner or later. The answer was she didn't know. She didn't have a single clue about that. She did tell Tanya, for right now, she was absolutely done with Ty for the time being.

She went through too much with that guy. She came to far forward, to go back now. Things cannot go back to the way things used to be. Dana took it like this, she had and enjoyed the great times she had with Ty. They created three precious and wonderful children, together. Who means, the world to her. She will always be grateful about that. She respects, the great times they spent together.

She looks at it now as being a learning experience That was the past. Dana was looking forward to her nice bright future that was ahead for her. Tanya and Dana got off the phone. Each ending the conversation with, they needed to get up with one another eventually. Hang out one day. Also, they needed to stay in contact. Unfortunately, with both of their busy schedules.

It would be hard for them to meet up. They did promise to each other regardless, of what. That they will be, meeting up again, in the near future. They vowed they'll make sure about that. Tanya made sure she had the whole story together. So, when she goes to pay Ty a visit, she has it all together. Tanya went to pay Ty a visit a couple of days later.

When she got inside the prison. She signed her name in the book. The prison guard escorted her to the visiting room. The prison guards brought Ty out from the back, shortly after. As he sat there cuffed to the chair in the visiting room. She touches his hand. Then she began to tell him, everything. Everything that Dana had told her.

Whatever questions he may have to ask her, she was prepared to answer them. She tells him, that Dana had a new man in her life. Plus, Dana was happy with him. Ty didn't budge. He continued to listen, calm, cool and collect. Tanya wore a tight skirt with a tight blouse. Like how she always looked. Whenever she went to pay Ty a visit. As she spoke about the information she acquired from Dana.

Ty was listening. Also, stirring at Tanya. He was checking out her body. He looks at her breast in her tight blouse. The way her breast looked like they were going to pop out of her blouse. Then he began to wonder how did she get into that skirt she had on. He noticed how the light in the prison visiting room shined on her legs as she has them crossed.

He kept on complimenting
Tanya on the way she was
looking. As she spoke, he
stirred. At this stage for
Ty, he hadn't seen nor
heard a woman up and close
in years. The last time he
saw a woman, was the last
time he saw Tanya. She
told him, that his kids liked
Dana's new friend. Ty's
whole attitude changed. He
sat there chained to the
chair, in disbelief. About
that information, right
there.

He took that as a straight up violation and disrespect. He had a stuck, stupid look on his face. For the moment. Still he wanted to hear know more. More information about his family. Especially, his kids. When Tanya told him, that Dana and his kids went into a shelter. After Dana stopped working. Tanya kept going. She dwelt on the fact, that Dana had Ty's children homeless.

She was downing Dana
every chance she got. Until
Ty told her, he didn't
agree with everything that
she was saying about Dana.
When it came down to the
working aspect. He knew
something must of, have
happened. Dana wasn't
reckless like that. He
defended her on that part.
But his kids being
homeless. Having to go into
a city shelter.

That's what got Ty extremely pissed off. Because he had no knowledge of this. If he would have known. He would have done something about it. Quickly, he showed Tanya he wasn't fazed by it. He began to look at her, while he began to lick his lips. Tanya was looking at his muscular body, that was bulging outside of his jail suit. She uncrosses her legs.

Then she crosses them to
the other side. She
couldn't help it. she had to
touch his face. He smelles
her sweet-smelling
perfume. When she touches
his face. The correction
officer wanted to
intervene. But instead, the
officer chilled. He let them
rock a little bit. Ty was
grateful for the news, he
received from Tanya. He
was always grateful, she
came to pay him a visit.

After, their visiting time was up. Ty told Tanya, thanks, and that she was his main girl. she asks him, was she? He repeated what he said in the first place. Yes, you're my main girl. Tanya told him, he would never have to worry about her, leaving him. She will always stand by his side. She will always be his main girl. She smiled. Then she told him, he was her main guy as well. She went on to say, she couldn't wait until he was able to get out of prison. So, she could show him, how she felt about him. They looked at each other, directly into each other's eyes. They both got up from the table. Then they walked away from one another. Ty turned back around as the prison guard began to escort him back inside of lock up. He watches Tanya's butt as she walks away in the opposite direction.

Before she left the prison grounds. She made sure, she put some in his commissary. Money on the books for Ty. Like she always did. Then she made her way back to the city, from upstate New York.

chapter 7

The first couple of months, on the job police officer Bridge was still trying to figure out Officer Nickels. Plus, it took time for him to get used to his new environment. Officer Nickels was making adjustment of having a new partner and all. Officer Nickels spends this same time, explaining to Officer Bridge, the reasons why? He didn't want a new partner.

He talks about his reasons why he felt that way. The main reason was what happened many years prior. After his partner, Officer Smith died. After his partner's murder, he rode solo. The department allowed him to do so. Which made him happy. First and foremost, he didn't have to worry about the next man or woman, getting murdered on his watch, again.

He made it clear, he had nothing against his new issued partner. He just didn't want anyone's blood on his hands. When he joined the police force several years ago. At first, all he wanted to do was make a difference. But he wanted to be honest. Mostly, all he ever received on the job was headaches and heartaches. The money wasn't all of that. It did pay the bills. The risks were high.

Years ago, at first, he
didn't like the way his old
partner conducted business.
Even though, he still
respected him. He first
thought, his old partner's
tactics were crazy. To do
this type of work. He tells
Officer Bridge, a couple of
stories about his old
partner, Office Smith. He
remembers how Officer
Smith riffled many people's
feathers. Still, Officer
Smith was a Hella, of a
cop.

One of the best that ever done it. When he died, he died a hero. What still got under Officer Nickels skin. Was the fact, no one ever solved the bank case. The case Officer Smith got murdered in. He vowed that one day, that case will be solved. Right now, he didn't have the jurisdiction to pursue the case any further. It was now classified as a cold case.

As Officer Nickels drove and spoke, Officer Bridge was taking it all in, what he was saying. Officer Nickels drove the police car throughout the neighborhood, they were assigned to patrol. While Officer Nickels was driving, he came to a stop sign. He took a good look at his new partner. Officer Nickels was extremely good at, remembering faces.

Officer Bridge reminded him of a face, he saw before. When Officer Smith stopped at a traffic light. He tells Officer Bridge, he looks like someone, he encountered before. But he didn't know where or why? He did go on to say, the person he had in mind, was on the other side of law. Officer Nickels begins to question Officer Bridge's about his whereabouts for the last 5 years.

Officer Bridge didn't understand, why was he asking these weird questions to him. He thought maybe, Officer Nickels was paranoid, for some weird reason. Officer Bridge told Officer Nickels, he was overseas fighting a war for the country. It wasn't hard to tell Officer Bridge was completely offended. He reached into his back-pants pocket.

He pulls out his wallet. He showed his partner his military I.D. He told officer Nickels that everyone wasn't a criminal. He reminds him, that he took the same oath as him. Which is to serve and protect. That's when it finally clicked into officer Nickels' brain. He realized, he was being a jerk. Because everyone has someone who looks like, them.

Officer Bride understood where Officer Nickels was coming from. He told Officer Nickels that he no hard feelings toward him. He also, knew that one-day Officer Nickels will regain trust in people. He knew the feeling, all too well. Once upon a time, he felt the same way towards people. He had to adopt to civilian life. Knowing everyone wasn't the enemy.

He had to remind himself on a daily basis, about this very fact. And that was an everyday process. Officer Bridge began to tell Officer Nickels how he felt, and things he saw and encountered, overseas fighting in a war. A war, he was just in. Officer Nickels was simply amazed by what Officer Bridge has gone through and has done. While serving this country.

Officer Nickels found a
new respect for his new
partner. The war stories
Officer Bridge talked
about. Officer Nickels
knew Officer Bridge had
lost a great deal of friends
in the war overseas.
Officer Nickels asked
Officer Bridge was he new
in New York city. Bridge
responded with, "yeah",
"something like that."
As they were finally able
to break the ice.

They were able to get to know, one another better. Officer Nickel and Officer Bridge got along very well after they gained a true understanding of each other. Once they realized they had so much in common. They became like the blues brothers. The black version. They were like the same guy inside, just with different bodies. They even approach things in similar ways.

When the commanding Officer asks Officer Nickels about, how he felt about his new partner. Nickels let the commanding officer know that everything was going great. Funny enough, when the commanding officer asked Officer Bridge the same question he got the same answer. They had no complaints about one another. They made a perfect team.

The commanding Officer was happy with the connection. Because it was very difficult to find a partner for Officer Nickels. When the higher ups, the police brass asked Bridge about Nickels as a precaution of Nickels current mental status. Bridge told them he was fine. Plus, he was a good partner for him. The police vehicle of their choice was a ran-down beat up old fashioned, unmarked squad car. Only the two of them would like a piece of trash like that. Without their knowledge, they were issued a new police cruiser. The police department made the change during the weekend. During their down time. Monday morning is when Officers Nickel and Bridge found out about the change. Neither one of them were happy with the change. They spend most of the morning at the mechanic shop.

They were persistent about what they wanted. And all they wanted was their old beat-up police car back. The mechanic laughed at the two Officers. He gave them a look. A look like they both was crazy. He couldn't get over the fact, that they were dead serious. They really wanted that piece of junk of a car back. He pointed at the ran-down beaten up police car in the corner of the police mechanic shop.

The Officers both motioned, yes to the car he was pointing at. They really wanted their car back. The mechanic pointed again, just trying to be funny. Making sure they were talking about that ran down police car. Again, they agreed, that's the car they wanted. They were dead serious about what they wanted. The head mechanic thought about it, for a moment.

Then he was like, you know something, you could have that piece of junk. Nickels and Bridge was happy. They thanked the mechanic for understanding. The mechanic really didn't understand. He didn't want to go back and forth, with these, police officers. He had other police vehicles to fix. He was up to his neck with police vehicles that needed to be worked on. He was only agreeing to get them out of his face.

The mechanic says to them, not so fast. He could have their vehicle up in running in the morning. Officer Nickels looks at his watch. Officer Bridge looks at the big wall clock in the mechanic's shop. Then they looked at the mechanic. They reminded the mechanic that it was only 10:00am in the morning. He explained that he had some work to do on it.

For now, they would have to drive the car they were assigned. The new police cruiser. Nickels and Bridge made it clear to the mechanic, only if they had to? They weren't happy about that. They knew they didn't have any choice in the matter. They'll have to deal with it for one day. They didn't move, until it was confirmed they were getting the police car of their choice in the morning.

The mechanic walks from the officers, he had other cars to deal with. The officers walk out. And got into the new police patrol car they were assigned to. They drove away, they went about their business. They began their normal daily routines. The day went slow to fast. But, not fast enough, as they wanted it to be. Just an average Monday.

Chapter 8

Summertime in the city
that never sleeps. Lil Ty
asks his mom about working
this summer. He really
wanted to get a summer
job. Dana was like, why
not? She saw nothing wrong
with that. Lil Ty was
starting to become
independent. Dana really
liked the fact. Plus, she
figured out, that it would
be a good thing for him.
First, that would keep him
out of trouble and off the
streets.

Most kids at 17 years old just wanted to hang out, and ask for things. For him to want to take the initiative to actually, want to work a job. It was not only a good thing. In, fact it was a great thing. He kind of, reminded her of herself working at the soda shop, back in the days. How it all got started. As she reminisces, she smiled and chuckled. Kudos to him.

Lil Ty starts to look for a summer job. He begins to look everywhere, after school. He started his job search a few weeks before school let out for the summer. He went to the mall. Stores far and near home. He experienced, what it felt like to think you're going to get the job, but unfortunately, you don't. That didn't stop him. He kept on with his search.

He realized, it was harder than what he thought it was going to be. Dana gave him a couple of job leads. That would be perfect for his age. She suggests, that he try to look for work in supermarkets, fast food restaurants industries. She felt like that would be right up his ally. Every morning on his way to school, while he walks to the train station. He always walks past this candy store.

The candy store was a couple of feet away from the train station staircase. Sometimes he would go in there to get a soda or some gum. Before he continues to go and catch the train, to get to school. The candy store, he thought nothing extra about. His job search got a little wider and a little bigger. He applied for a job at the movie theater. At school he went to his guidance counselor.

His guidance counselor sends him to the job search counselor. Who dealt with summer jobs. She also helps students get their working papers. He went to the job counselor's office. She tells him, she was sorry. Because all the summer youth job was all filled up. She did help him get his working papers. She told him, he had come too late. She advises him to come earlier the next year.

He should had come a couple of months, before school let out for the summer break. She didn't want to leave him, without giving him some type of assistance. She suggests, he should check out places like, amusement parks, museums, also messenger positions. He took her advice. He tried out all the places, she told him to check out. A couple of places called him back.

The outcome yet again, lead to dead ends. It was one thing or another, was the reason they didn't hire him. He told his mother about his bad luck, with finding a job. She advises him to keep on looking. That's how the job, market is. The day you give up. The day you stop trying and looking. Will be the same day, you could of have had a job.

He kept on looking, because he saw that's what his mother, wanted him to do. One of his classmates told him to him to check out the pharmacy. One day on his way to school, he passes the candy store on the corner. He noticed a help wanted sign in the store window. His first reaction was, nah, they're not going to hire him. He wasn't taking the sign seriously. That same sign been in the store window for a while.

He remembers, he knew a girl in his school who works there. At lunchtime, he asks the girl about it. she said they were hiring. She declined, when he asks her out on a date. Even though he got turned down, for one thing. He did get the information, he wanted to know. On his way coming home from school, the next day. After he got off the train, he decides to go into the candy store.

His thoughts for the moment was, why not? He got nothing to lose. But he has so much to gain. He went inside the candy store. He walks up to the girl, he knew from school. he asks her, could he speak to the store manager. His friend from school, couldn't leave the cash register. So, she asked one of her co-workers to go to the back to get the store manager.

While he waited to speak to the store manager. She asks the pretty girl from school would she liked to go out on a date with him, again. She told him like she told him a day ago. Which was no. With the answer he got back from her. He just smiles at her. She smiles back. Coming from the back of the store, was this beautiful older, young mature woman. She asks him, could she help him with something.

He asked her for a job application. At first, she was acting funny towards him. Like, she really didn't want to be bothered. She went into one of the cash register draws. She pulls out an application. She places it in his hands. He asked her could he take the application home to fill it out, and bring it back the next day. She said sure why not?

Before he left, he asks the manager, what was the job description? He felt like asking that type of a question, made him feel and look more important. When he asks her, that question She gave him an aggravated look, like he was over doing it. She still, acted like he was bothering her. He thought, maybe the reason, she had an attitude was because she was having a bad day, or something.

He didn't think too much about it. She gave him a half ass break down about the job, and what it consisted of. Beyond all, of the mood swings. She did like the fact, that he asked her an intelligent question. She advised him to bring the application with a couple of other forms of I.D.'s, when comes back tomorrow. She told him good luck. Also, she hopes to see him the next day.

He smiles and tells her to have a nice day. She smiles back. Then she went back, to the back of the store, where the offices were located at. He left out the store and went on his way. He felt like he made, some type of progress. He had a good feeling about this particular job. When Stuy came to the candy store, the next day. He went inside of his office. That was located at the back of the store.

Next to the manager's office. The store manager knocks on his office door. He tells her to come in. He was reading the store supply reports. That was placed on his desk. She came in after she was told to do so. She has in her hands a bunch of papers. She places each document on Stuy's desk. Which consisted of a bunch of bills. That came in the mail.

She also places the new applicants, applications on the other side of the desk. She wanted to know his input on the new applicants, applications. That was there. She had four positions to be filled. 2 full-time, 2 part-time. He went over the applications. There were about 15 applications there. She broke it down. Who and why, she was thinking about hiring for the summer.

She already had made up her mind. She wanted to look out for a couple of her family members with a summer job. He asked her, where was the money at. The money the store made on that day. He tells her to get the money together, because he wanted to deposit it, in the bank. He wants to get to the bank, before the bank closes for the night.

She calls one of the store workers on laod speaker, to come to the back office. She orders the worker, to go, clean out all the store's cash registers. After the manager receives, all the money. she had all the money the day before, in the store's safe. She took that money out. She combines the money with the money, she counts from the cash registers. she comes up with a complete sum of money.

She comes back into his office. She passes him an index card with the total sum of money on it. The sum was all the money, the store has made, for the last couple of days. Then she went into her back pocket. When she remembers she has one more application to go over with Stuy. He was watching what she did. He quickly asks her, what was that?

She tells him, it was nothing. It wasn't that serious. She told him, it was some kid, who she felt like, didn't qualify for any of the positions. For some weird reason, maybe off of instinct, today out of all days, he decides to ask his store manager, to let him see the application. Before she threw it away. She hands over the application to him. He reads the name on the application.

The name on the application was Ty-Rome Medina. Once he read it, he began to smile. She asks him, why was he smiling for? She couldn't help but notice how his face lit up. He explains to her, the person who name appears on the application, had the same name as his older brother. To make a joke out of it. He was like, why would his brother be looking for a job, over there, out of all places, why here?

He begins to laugh. She laughs also. She tells him, that he was crazy. Then he read the birth date on the application. She told him, the age of the applicant. He knew exactly who it was. She kept on laughing. She asks him, to give her back the application, so she could throw the application away. Because it was nothing to her. That's what came out her mouth next. After she said, what she said.

She notices, he wasn't laughing with her anymore. She was the only one, who found humor out of her joke. Quickly, she changes her facial expression. She took a more serious look on her face. Especially, when he told her to set up an interview with this young man. Also, he would like to meet this young man. She went on to say, "For what?"

She reminds him, she was already going to hire enough people, to fill all the new positions. That meant no positions were available. She told him, she already picked, who she felt was best qualified for the job, in her head. He understood, what she was saying. Still, that didn't matter to him. He insists, she sets up an appointment with the young man. She knew, she couldn't disagree.

It wouldn't be a smart choice to disagree with the owner of the whole establishment. He went on to say, better yet, hire him, after his interview. She said sure, to whatever he wanted. After that what was said, she didn't waste any time. She called Ty-Rome's home. Dana answers the phone. Cindy the store manager asks to speak to Ty-Rome Medina.

Dana lets her know, he was unavailable to come to the phone, at the present, moment in time. Cindy asks Dana, could she leave him a message? Dana wanted to know what was this pertaining to? She tells her, she represents a job that Ty-Rome applied for. Dana was okay with that. Cindy gave her the message. Dana let her know, that Ty-Rome will get the message.

When Lil Ty got home.
Dana gave him the
message. The message
consisted of the date and
time of his interview at the
candy store. Dana was the
first person to congratulate
him. On his new job. Back
at the candy store. After
Cindy made the phone call.
Stuy felt like business was
done, for the day. He
offered Cindy a ride home.
They closed the store for
the night.

He let her know, he had to make one stop before he took her home. She was okay with that. While he was taking her home, she didn't understand, what was going on. She went to her office to get her purse and jacket. She met up with him outside. Where he was waiting in his car. When she came out of the store. Stuy got out of his car, to press the button to activate the automatic gate system.

They watched the store
gates go down, in the car.
Then they drove off. She
has a slight attitude
because of what he said.
He tells her, he was taking
her home. She really didn't
know, where any of that
was coming from. She
couldn't figure out what
was going through
Stuyvesant's mind.
Normally, when he offers
her a ride home. After
they closed the store.

She winds up spending the night at his place. She caught on to it. when he told her, he'll be taking, her home, to her place. She wasn't expecting that. Now, she wants to know, who the hell was this kid? Why did his eyes light up, when he saw that kid's name? She was thinking about it the whole ride home. She didn't say anything about it. She just thought about it.

While in route, taking her home. He did mention to her, that he couldn't wait to tell his sister about it. He really didn't dwell on it. Cindy wasn't going to ask, either. She just left it alone. He did, just what he said, he was going to do. He dropped her home, after he made his stop at the bank. Then he went, on his way home. The first thing he did, when he reached home.

He calls his sister on the phone. He wants to tell her, who he thought applied for a position at his candy store. Plus, he wanted to make sure, he was thinking that kid, was the right kid, he thought he was. Once he told his Betty about the news. She was thrilled to hear about it. She confirmed, that it was Ty's son name. She told him, it had to be him.

Knowing this fact, she told Stuy, she couldn't wait to tell their big bro., about it. The main thing she wanted to know, was did he hire him for the job? He laughed at the question. He said of course, he hired him. They talked about the fact that they didn't see Lil Ty in years. To them, Dana and her kids fell off the face of the earth, when Big Ty went to prison. The had lost contact with Dana.

But, they were surely glad they were about to come across them again. Now, they'll be able keep in contact with them for good. When it came down to the candy store. Betty took care of the paperwork, and pay roll. Which made it a perfect, for Lil Ty to be working there. Betty continues to laundry Ty's money, from the bank heist, through the candy store. She's been doing this for years now.

By now millions have been
deposit into the bank.
When Ty called Betty from
prison. He had a lot of
questions, that he needed
to be answered. Betty had
some new news of her own,
to tell him about. Ty didn't
waste no time beating
around the bush, his phone
time was limited. He asked
Betty, did she know
anything about Dana and
the kids being in the
shelter?

Also, why they had to go into the shelter? He wanted and needed to know. Plus, when was she going to tell him about this. She explains to her older brother, she had no clue about what he was talking about. She didn't even know it went down like that. After he went to prison, a couple of months later, they lost contact with Dana. She admits, she saw them, a couple of times.

Then something must have happened, that was completely out of her control. Because after she tried to visit them. She tried to reach out to Dana. When she called the phone number Dana gave her. The phone was disconnected. She never heard or saw them again. Betty was sad to hear about that. She let him know, how she felt about this. She was very unhappy and upset to hear about it.

The news Ty told her, broke her heart. She tells her brother, if she would have known. She would have, had to put this matter into her own hands. He knew his sister wasn't bullshitting about that. He heard it all in her voice. She quickly got herself together for the moment on the phone. She knew phone time was limited, for Ty. She told Ty what she needed to tell him. She let him know, that Lil Ty came

to the candy store looking
for part-time job. Ty
asked her, what has
happened with that? He
went on to say, if Lil Ty
needs a job, then he should
get the job he wants.
Before he could go, on and
on about it. She tells him,
Stuy did give Lil Ty the
job. Ty told Betty, what
he wanted her to do. How
he wanted to give Lil Ty
some money. The amount of
money he felt like his son

needs, at this stage of his life. He thinks up a plan, on how Lil Ty could get the money without anyone knowing about it. Knowing what's really going down. Betty followed his instructions. She knew what she had to do. Lil Ty told his mother, how the interview went well, and that day, he got the job. Dana was so excited to hear about it. When she asks him which store location?

He tells her, the one by the train station. Lil Ty began to tell her the store's address and everything. He forgot, she knew exactly where it was at. After, he had already told her so. Nevertheless, she allows him to carry on. She stood there truly proud of her son. She was okay with it, she did mention, she would be checking the place out, one of these days.

Lil Ty shows his mother, his brother and sister, his new uniform shirt. Dana felt like, he deserves a celebration. She let him know, just one thing. Under one condition, every once in a while, he buys something for his brother and sister. He looks at Will and Myesha, then he smiles and then agrees to her terms. Everyday afterschool Lil Ty went to work at the candy store.

The store manager Cindy,
asked him where did he
know the store owner
from? He gave her an
honest look. So, when he
told her, he didn't know, it
was an honest look on his
face, because he really
didn't know. He really
meant it. To the best of
his knowledge, he never
saw the owner of the candy
store before. He felt a
little embarrassed and
uncomfortable.

Because he never met anyone, who ever owned anything, in his life, before. Let alone, a big store like this one. The one he works at. He felt a little out of place. Ashamed, but he didn't show it. Cindy took a long deep look at him. She saw he really didn't have a clue, on what she was asking him about. He didn't know anything that was going on. Still, she kept on coming to him, with the bullshit.

Even though, she didn't
know what was going on,
either. Her first instinct,
her so-called woman's
intuition, had her to
believe, that Stuy was
messing around with the
young guy's mother, behind
her back. Cindy was the
jealous type. She had it all
figured out, in her head.
Thinking maybe his mother
wanted Stuy to herself.
That was the only thing
that made sense inside of
her head.

She felt like Stuy was acting strange towards her, when it came down to this kid. She wanted to know why? What was so special about this particular kid. That became her mission, her obsession. Her lone purpose and mission. She went over Lil Ty's job with him, as she trains him. She was going to make it her business, to make sure he has the worst things to do on this job.

Stuy went on vacation for a couple of weeks. She was already mad, because he didn't take her with him. So, Cindy decides to give Lil Ty so much work. That he would have no choice, but to quit. Before, Stuy came back from his vacation. She wanted him to be gone before that. Stuy and Lil Ty still haven't met up as of yet. Even though, Lil Ty didn't know who the owner was. Or, even cared to know.

The young man just wanted
to work, every day,
afterschool. All he wants
to do, was to put a little
money in his pockets. He
worked and worked, until
he got sore and tired.
Cindy made sure of that.
He didn't have any pleasant
days at the job. His first
couple of weeks, were
brutal to him. When he got
home, Dana noticed, how
drained and tired Lil Ty
was.

With him dealing with school and work, she was really, ready to tell him, she didn't think it was such a good idea after all. She really wanted to tell him this. When she did confront him about it. He did acknowledge the fact, that he was tired and drained. He did explain to mother, that he wanted to do this, also it was coming towards the end of the school year.

He'll be alright for right now. When school ends for the year. He'll be able to get the proper rest that was much needed. Dana asks him, where did he get this no quit attitude from? He smiled and told his mother, he learned not to quit or give up mentally. Which, he got that from his momma. Lil Ty smiled at Dana, his mother. Dana smiled back with a tear in her eyes.

Myesha asked her mommy, why she was crying for? Dana told her because she was happy. "Them tears of joy." She said, as she hugs and kisses Myesha. Myesha had a puzzled look on her face. The next reaction from her, was to, just leave that one alone. Dana saw how determined Lil Ty was about working. Making his own money. She was so proud of him. Will wanted to get a job too.

Dana flat out told him, No! He was too young. She told him, in a couple of years and better grades, then they could talk about it. Myesha also asked could she get a job. Dana didn't feel like going back and forth with her little behind. So, she decided to create a job for Myesha to do. Myesha's job was to make sure the house was cleaned. The kitchen sink, the bathroom and her room had to be clean, at all times. Myesha sat there with her cute self. She had the nerve to ask her mommy, "how much does the job pays?" She said with a silly, cute smirk on her face. Dana tells her the pay rate and job description. Myesha had a question about the pay. She asks her mommy, was that her final offer? Dana said to Myesha, well you can take it, or leave it? The choice is yours.

Dana starts laughing afterwards. Myesha had the nerve to try to figure out how much, she'll be getting paid. She was trying to calculate her money on her fingers. She came up with what was owed to her. Funny thing about this, was she had put in zero hours, into actually working. She wanted to get paid upfront. It just got funnier, by the moment. Dana looks at Myesha and says to her, "Girl Bye!"

Then they both began to laugh. Dana told her mother about it. Ms. Medina thought it was so cute. She tells, just about all her friends about the story, that Dana told her about. Everyone who heard it, thought it was cute too. After two weeks of hard labor, on the job. Lil Ty receives his first paycheck. And it wasn't pretty. Still, he was happy to get a paycheck.

When he opened his paycheck in front of Cindy. She watched and waited to see, what would be his response to it. Because she purposely cut some hours out of his paycheck. She thought that would make him mad. Upset enough, to make him give up and quit. That was the cherry on top of her cake. The cake he didn't eat, to her amazement. Since the school year was over.

He asks her could he get more hours a week at work. She quickly tells him, he should be happy with the hours, he was already getting. Because that was all the hours, he'll be getting. She made sure she added, if he didn't like it. He could always go somewhere else, too work. For all she cared. Again, she was waiting for a response. Still, she didn't receive one.

What he did ask her about, was what she wanted him to do for the day. What his assignment was going to be? She basically gave him all the work. It got so bad, while he did all the work. The rest of the workers gathered around and watched. Because they had nothing else to do. Most of them, thought it was funny. A few didn't understand, why was she doing that to him?

He just worked his job. He didn't feed into any of the silliness. It was so obvious, he couldn't help, but notice it. When the work day was over, he went to cash his check. That day he went home, with money in his pocket. Money, he earned himself. Oh, what a feeling that was for the young man. He gives his brother and sister 10 dollars apiece. They both was happy about that.

When Dana got home from work, Myesha ran up to her and shows her, what she got from her big brother. She tells her the news as soon as, she got into the door. Even before, Dana could take off her jacket and put the groceries on the kitchen counter. She sat the bags next to a pizza box. Dana asks them where was Lil Ty at? They both pointed at the bedroom.

Dana looks inside the pizza box. She saw it was a whole pizza pie inside of the box. That haven't been touched yet. Of course, you know Myesha was all in the business. Dana went to the boy's room. She wanted to talk, to Lil Ty. She wanted to tell him, that he did good. When she went inside the room. She saw Lil Ty was completely, knocked out, sleeping. He was out of it, fast asleep.

She looks at him, she places a sheet over him. And kisses his forehead. Like if he was her baby all over again. Well to her, he will always be her baby, no matter, how big or old he gets. She went back to the kitchen. Her and the other kids had a little pizza party on Lil Ty's expense. She made sure, she left a couple of slices of pizza for him. Just in case, he got up later and was hungry.

Dana liked everything Lil Ty did that night. She thought it was so sweet. Her only concern was why was he so tired? She couldn't understand it, he was only working at a candy store. How much work can he possibly be doing? That's what had her puzzled.

Chapter 9

When it became closing time at the candy store. The name of the candy store, was named Stuy's candy shop. Stuy's candy store wasn't just the average candy store. He purchased it several years ago. Since, the time he bought it, he has made it bigger and bigger. Which made it better and better. He expanded the store a couple of times. With the success of his first store, he was able to purchase a couple more stores across town. What started as an opportunity of a lifetime. He took full advantage of the opportunity that he was given. He found success out of it. With hard work and sacrifices, he made himself a nice small fortune. With all the work he had put into it. He well, deserves what was coming to him. He came to check up, on his headquarters, his main store, that evening.

Thinking he would get a chance to meet up with Lil Ty. When he arrived at the store. He walks up to Cindy and asks her, where was Ty-Rome at? She tells him, she sent him home, a little earlier. Her asks her why? She came up with a bull shit excuse. She told him, she was ready to fire him. Because he was lazy. He didn't want to work. Bottom line he wasn't cut out for this job.

Stuy told her, they will discuss this, after he uses the bathroom. As he walks in the bathroom. He checks the bathroom detail list. The list that indicates who cleaned the bathroom, a couple times a day. He notices that Lil Ty's name was all over the list, from little Ty's signature. After seeing that, he decides to do some more investigating for himself. He notices throughout the store.

All the duty list had Lil Ty's name, written all over all of them. So, Lil Ty being lazy, was pure bullshit to him. Once he gathered enough information, he walked up to Cindy. He asks her to meet him, in his office. That's where he began to question her. Questions, like what was everybody else doing, while Ty-Rome did all the work? Because Ty-Rome's name was on all the work list.

The next question was why Ty-Rome was doing all of that? Why she had the nerve to call him lazy? He couldn't understand that. Especially, when Lil Ty only worked there part-time. Cindy, just kept on with the excuses. He tells Cindy, he'll back tomorrow. He'll be back early the next day. He made it clear to her, she needs to make sure Ty-Rome was there, when he gets there.

She said fine. She couldn't understand why was this kid, so important to him. That remanded a mystery to her. Which made it all the reason for her to get to the bottle line of it all. The next day, Lil Ty came to work usual. With no idea of what has taken place, the evening before. When he got there, he begins to work, his first tour of duties. It wasn't hard to tell. He was already extremely tired.

Cindy asks him again. Did he know who the store owner was? Again, he replied with, No! He didn't know who the store owner was. He didn't understand why she kept on asking him the same questions. He remained very confused about that. She gave him a bunch of work to do. She lets him know, the store owner wanted to see him, personally. He asks her why?

She tells him, that
probably the store owner
wants to fire him, himself.
He couldn't understand,
what he did wrong? He did
everything that was asked
of him to do. Still, he
guesses, it just wasn't good
enough. Still, he wasn't
going out without a fight.
He wasn't no quitter. So,
he continues to work as
hard as he possibly could.
He asks the manager for a
break.

She just wanted him to get back to work. She even threatens to fire him, right there on the spot, if he didn't get back to work. And finish what he was doing. Lil Ty starts feeling awkward. The whole moment was awkward. The way she was acting towards him was way beyond awkward. He really wasn't feeling that well, that day. He felt terrible, maybe it was something he ate.

He begins to sweat. All he was asking for, was a couple of minutes to gather himself together. Since Cindy, the store manager was so persistence, Lil Ty continues to work through it. Luckily, for Lil Ty, it was just gas. After he passes some gas. After a while, it made him feel a whole lot better. He still was worried about what the store owner wanted him for.

He had no time to think about that. He had so much work to do. He started calculating how many hours, he worked for this work-time period. He figures out, at least, he could get a pair of sneakers out of it, with his last check at work. The way his co-workers were acting weird towards him. It was plain to see, even to Ty-Rome. He prepares himself to hear the news

everyone was waiting to
hear. Truth be told, he
was just happy to have had
a chance, to work a job.
He was young and happy
about that. He felt like, he
done proved his point. The
point, he wanted to prove
to himself. That was all,
that really matters to him.
He could work a job, make
his own money. Stuy, came
to the store as planned. He
came even earlier than he
told Cindy.

He walks around the store undetected. He walks up to the cashier. He asks her where was Ty-Rome at. Before she answered him, she asks him, why was he going to fire Ty-Rome for? Stuy's reaction was, why would he do a thing like that? She explains to him, that it was a rumor going around the store, that he would. He also tells her, not tell anyone, that he was there.

Then he went on to say,
you shouldn't believe
everything you hear. She
answers him with, Ty-Rome
is in the bathroom cleaning,
Mr. Bridge. He made his
way to the store's public
bathroom. He opens the
Men's bathroom door. And
there he was, Lil Ty. Lil
TY was moping the men's
bathroom floor. He calls
Ty-Rome, Lil Ty. He
wanted to see Lil Ty's
reaction to it.

Quickly, he turns around to see who was calling his name. Lil Ty wasn't used to someone calling him, Lil Ty that he didn't know. Stuy asks him, did he know, who he was? Lil Ty figures out, that he must be the store owner. So, he says, "Yeah," "you must be the store owner." Before Lil Ty allows Stuy, to say anything else, he acknowledges, that he knew why he was there.

And what he was going to
do. All Lil Ty wanted to
know, was why? With all
the things, the manager
made him do. What else
could he had possibly done,
to change the predicament,
he finds himself in. Stuy
looks at him. Then he asks
him, was he finished? Lil
Ty watches and waits, to
hear what the man has to
say. Stuy starts off with,
besides him being the store
owner, did he know, who he
was?

Lil Ty really, didn't know how to respond. He was wondering why was this man asking him, all of these questions. Stuy tells him, that he remembers him as a little boy. A baby to be exact. At this point, Lil Ty became curious, to know where he knew this guy from. And where this guy knew him from. Lil Ty knew his parents knew, a whole lot of people. Still, he had difficulty picturing this man's face.

He tells, Mr. Bridge he really didn't know, who he was. And where he knew him from. Finally, Stuy let Lil Ty know, that he was his uncle. Lil Ty was shocked to hear that news. It was an unreal moment for him. Stuy told him that his father was his older brother. Lil Ty knew all his mother's side of the family. He didn't know too many people from his father side of the family.

The only one, he kind of knew, was his aunt Betty. That's when Stuy let him know, that his aunt Betty was his younger sister. Lil Stuy stood there with the mop in his hands. He stood there shocked to say the least. He asks Lil Ty how he was being treated, working there. Lil Ty acknowledges, that the work was hard. He was okay with that. Ms. Cindy was mean and hard.

He figured out, she was like that towards everybody. Well, he assumed. Stuy asks Lil Ty to follow him to his office. They walked out of the bathroom. All the people who works there stopped, what they were doing. Stirring, trying to see what was going on. What was going to happen.

Everyone just knew, Ty-Rome was going to get fired.

Lil Ty follows his uncle to his uncle's office. He told Lil Ty to have a seat. He asks his nephew did he want something to drink. Lil Ty wanted a soda. Stuy bought him a soda. Stuy told him to stay in his office, while he went to take care of some other business. Lil Ty stayed seated in the office, like he was told to do. Stuy left the store for a moment.

While he was gone, one of
the nosy workers mentions
the fact to Cindy, that
Ty-Rome was in Mr.
Bridge's office. Plus, the
fact that Mr. Bridge had
left the store. Once she
heard that news. All hell
broke loose. Cindy went to
the owner's office, where
Ty-Rome was at. She
didn't waste any time at
all. She asks Lil Ty, why
and what, was he doing
back here in these offices.

Before he could answer her. She ordered him to go back to work. After that has been said, she gave him a bunch of vigorous jobs to do. He didn't feel like arguing with her. So, he did what she asks him to do. When Stuy came back to the store. He went straight to the back, where his office was located at. He went to check on Lil Ty. He opens his office door, and Lil Ty wasn't there.

He walks back out to the
floor of the store. Lil Ty
was nowhere to be found.
Stuy didn't understand why
his nephew left his office.
He began to search all the
aisles in the store, looking
for him. He didn't see him,
he couldn't find him. He
went to Cindy, to ask her,
where was Ty-Rome at.
Cindy flat out told him, she
had caught Ty-Rome
snooping around his office.

She let it be known, she didn't trust him. She went on to say, if she was Stuy, she would fire him immediately, over what has taken place. She advises him to check everything in his office, if anything was missing, she thinks they should call the police. She stated again, she really wants to fire him. She was just waiting for Stuy to come back. He asks her again where was Ty-Rome?

For that moment, that's all he wanted to know. That's all he really cared about. She tells him, he was outback doing the garbage duties. Stuy went outside to the back of the store. Where the dumpsters were located at. He saw Lil Ty in a mountain of garbage bags and containers. He calls his name. Lil Ty ignored him. He just kept on doing his job. It wasn't hard to tell that his nephew was upset.

Just off the way Lil Ty was acting. That made Stuy extremely angry. He rushes back into the store. He calls Cindy to his office. She tells him, it's something about that kid, that, she really didn't like. That kid has been nothing but trouble from the day, he started working there. She knew one thing for sure, she couldn't wait until that kid was gone. Gone out of their lives.

So, things could get back to being normal. Stuy looks at her, he says to her, "Oh really!" Then he asks her some major questions. He asked Cindy, did she remember the big picture on the wall at his house. The picture of his older brother Ty-Rome. She already had a slight attitude, because she was all worked up, for what reason? Only she knew that.

So, she replies with a yeah, whatever. He asks her, guess what? He said it with a not so pleasant tone, in his voice. "You know that little baby boy", "my brother was holding in his arms?" "My nephew Ty-Rome!" Again, she said, "yeah!" Cindy starts to put one and one together. Her mouth became wide opened. All she could say was, "oh my God!" "Ty-Rome that works here", "is Lil Ty-Rome in the picture?"

She stood there, her face turned red, with the look of stupidity, written across it. All she was able to say, was she was so sorry. And she didn't know. Stuy went to tell her, that she had King Ty's son working in the garbage. He calls Cindy crazy. He let her know, if his brother finds out about this. Lord, knows what he'll do to him. When he gets out of prison.

Cindy remains there speechless. Stuy told her to leave his office. Cindy didn't know what to say or do. Clearly, Stuy was totally disgusted with her. Cindy left the office with an overwhelming sense of guilt, written all over her face. She didn't know what to do at this, point in time. Not only was Stuy her boss, the owner of the store. He also was her love interest.

She decides to leave
everything alone for the
moment. She felt like, she
had done enough already.
She knew, she messed up
big time, on so many levels.
The sad part about it was.
She didn't have a single
clue, on how to make any
of this better. Right then
and there, she realizes,
she was having a very bad
day. Lil Ty came back into
the store after doing the
garbage detail.

He went up to Cindy, to ask her, what did she want him to do next. She notices that he was upset and embarrassed. All the workers did want to work next him, because he smelled like garbage. They didn't want to be near him. They all was making jokes about him. Like everything he was going through, was funny. Lil Ty did feel the pressure.

But he was determined not to be bothered by other, people's nonsense. She offers him a break. He just looks at her. He was disgusted with her. But his mother taught him to always respect his elders. He tries his best not to show it. He politely declined the offer. He told her, he just wanted to work. He wouldn't even look at her, in her face. His eyes were to the ground.

She gave him something to do. Something that wasn't that hard to do. She clearly, saw he didn't want to be bothered. Stuy was in his office. He remained there broken hearted. Because that's not how, he wanted any of it, to go down. Lil Ty just couldn't wait until the day was over. All he wanted to do, was to go home. Lil Ty worked until closing time. That's when his shift was over.

As closing time came near, Stuy came out of his office. He came up to Cindy and Lil Ty. He offers Lil Ty a ride home. Lil Ty looks at him, then he looks at her. He told his uncle, no thank you, to a ride home. He tells him, he rather, walk home. Both Stuy and Cindy could smell the garbage smell coming Lil Ty's work uniform. As he walks out of his uncle's eyesight.

All the long, Cindy's eyes were on Stuy, the whole time. Stuy told her, he'll see her tomorrow. Then he got into his car and drove off. Cindy made her way to the subway. Cindy felt really, bad about what had happened that day. She felt bad about how she treated that young man. She understood, she had no right to treat him like that. She was very ashamed of her actions.

That was her thoughts on it. As she rode the subway train home. Even when she got home, she continued to feel bad. She tried to call Stuy. But she got no answer. She knew he was upset with her. She wasn't the only one, who felt some type of way, about that day. When Dana got home from work. She notices Lil Ty sitting on the living room couch, with his head down.

She could sense that something was bothering with him. She asks him, do he want to talk about it? He declined. Before she left him alone. He did say one thing. He told her, today, he met his uncle for the first time, to his knowledge. Dana asked him, how did that go? He went back to being silence. It was clear, he didn't want to talk about it. She let him know, if he did wants to talk about it, she'll be there to listen. She also, tells him, that she loves him. Then she left alone. She knew that was what he needed. The next day at work, Cindy offers him more hours, during the summer time. He agrees and accepts, what she was offering. Still, he wasn't trusting Cindy, the store manager. He made sure, he kept his guards up, at all time at work.

He just wants to work, and not be bothered. When his uncle came around to speak to him. He spoke back. Just like his mother taught him to do. But that was as far as it went. Stuy didn't know how to respond, to the way Lil Ty was acting towards him. He could tell the young man was disappointed from the whole situation. He really didn't want his nephew to feel that way.

Especially, knowing how his older brother, felt about him. He felt like he was letting his brother down. That's what made it even more depressing, because that was his brother's oldest child, feeling like that. Feeling like he wasn't wanted there. He knew, Lil Ty needs him in his life, right about now. Since, his father was locked away in prison.

Stuy knew some way, somehow, he had to make this better. No matter, what was the cost. He knew had to at least try. When Stuy spoke to his sister about what has taken place. Betty explains to her brother, that Lil Ty had the right, to feel the way he felt. The young man doesn't know his father's side of the family, all that well. Also, he's been through so much.

More than, anyone will ever know. From his father going in and out of jail. When his mother couldn't hold it down. So, they had to live in a shelter. Stuy knew, he couldn't possibly understand what his nephew has been through. Stuy listened and absorbed, what his sister was to say to him. Somethings he knew, others he never knew about. What made it shocking, to hear it now?

She went on to say, remember when daddy died, it was a struggle. Hard to trust people. Luckily, they had their big brother, Ty, to look out for them. He tells Betty, that's the reason, why he was feeling bad, over the way Lil Ty was being treated, indirectly. That was a major concern of his. He really didn't know how to approach the whole situation. He asks her, did she have any suggestions?

She first needed to know, what exactly did happen. All he could tell her was a brief account, of what he heard happened. To the best of his knowledge, he had heard Ty had some problems with one of the store managers. She asks him, which one was it? Who was they talking about? Then she pauses and thinks about it. She asks him, was it the store manager, that he was sleeping with?

He didn't want to say who it was. He had no choice, but to go ahead and agree with his sister on that one. Betty always felt like that chick, Cindy was bad for business. Stuy had nothing to say. All he could do was listen and agree with what Betty was saying on this matter. Because he knew deep down inside, it was true. He had to admit the only reason why he was paying attention, to the way she treats their employees, was due to the fact, that it was his nephew being treated in the same fashion. Betty was like, she wouldn't be surprised, if she did that to a lot more of his employees. More than they think. All because, she felt like she could just do that, because who she messes around with. But that was another story, that will be address on another day.

The main, focus was on their nephew. She let it be known, Ty knew Lil Ty works there. Stuy listens to what she just said, with his head hung on the other side of the phone call. She tells Stuy, that time heals all wounds. Give it some time, and everything will be alright. Stuy thoughts were, I hope so... They ended their phone conversation on that note. Betty had her own plans on

how she was going to make
her nephew happy. He'll be
happy when he receives his
next paycheck. She knew
that for sure. Lil Ty went
work the next day and the
next. When payday came
around. It started off as a
nice summer day. But with
a few surprises to it.
First, was the unexpected
guess who came to visit him
at work. Less than 2 hours
in, at work.

He looks up, and sees his mother and sister walking inside the candy store. Dana decides to pay Ty a visit at work. That's what she told him. Once they got face to face with him, he asks them, why were they there for? Cindy was looking at them, from a distance. She dared not, to come any closer. Dana told Lil Ty, they were there to get Myesha some candy.

Myesha looks around the candy store in amazement. Seeing so many, different kinds of candy to choose from. She was acts, like she was in Candy heaven. She kept on telling her mom, that it was so many candies to choose from. Myesha asks her big brother to help her choose some. Lil Ty looks at his mother. Dana reminds Myesha that Lil Ty was at work.

He can't stop working, just to help you baby girl. Things don't go like that. Remember your big brother has a job. Dana told Lil Ty, she'll be back, she wanted to take Myesha around the store. Lil Ty went back to work. Only, to be stopped by another unannounced guess, his aunt Betty. She was there to pick some paperwork and the payroll sheets from the office.

normally, she sends someone else to pick these things up for her. But today she decides to do it herself. When she walks inside the store Ty didn't see her, but she saw him. When she walks up to him, he looks up, and sees her. He stops work for a second time. He Remembers, his aunt. He got up and her a kiss on her cheek. She asks him, how was he feeling? He said, he was fine.

She also, tells him, she'll be back soon. Cindy stood behind the cash register, tries her best, to be out of sight, out of mind. As she was looks from a far. She was completely thrown off guard, that day. She hid with no luck. Betty went straight to her. She was watching Cindy all along. She wanted Cindy to go to the office, to get the company's time sheets for the week.

Betty follows her to the back to the office. Betty asks Cindy, was everything alright. She responds with, everything's fine. Betty was really asking about her nephew and her. Betty was trying to figure out what was the problem. Cindy told her, what had happened. Without Betty having to ask. Cindy began to explain, her actions towards Ty-Rome. Cindy made it clear, she had no idea, he was related to them. She acknowledges, she was wrong for her actions. Regardless, of whoever it was. She apologizes to Betty. Betty understood it could have been an honest mistake. Betty made sure Cindy understood, that Ty-Rome was her nephew. Plus, his father is the King. The king of all this, that she sees. She made this clear about all of that.

She tells Cindy, she better makes sure, this doesn't happen again. She wanted Cindy to understand this. She went to say, if it ever happens again, she won't be so friendly about it. Cindy became extremely nervous, to the point of being scared. She felt at ease, when Betty left the office. She was able to breathe again. Betty began to walk around the store.

The employees who worked there greeted Ms. Bridge. While walking the aisles of the store, she bumped into Dana and Myesha. Dana was talking to Lil Ty when Betty walks up to them. Myesha notices her aunt, she runs up to her and gives her a hug and a big kiss. Myesha was so happy to see her aunt. Betty told Myesha, her uncle owned this candy store. Myesha stood there for a moment.

Then her face lit up, and she said, "Wow!" She didn't know what to do, or how act with that information. That definitely made her day. Also, seeing her aunt as well. For a moment, she forgot she was in a store full of candy. Just only for a moment. A kid in a candy was music to a kid's ears. She was ready for some candy. Dana and Betty exchanges contact information.

So, they could keep in contact. Dana knew being in contact with Betty meant being in contact with Ty. Dana didn't mind the fact. Because that wasn't a bad thing. He was her children's father. When Cindy came out of the office. She was thinking that Betty had left the store, by then. But Betty didn't. Betty saw Cindy. So, she calls her over to where she was at with Dana and Lil Ty.

She wanted her to meet Ty-Rome's mother, and little sister. Cindy greets them. Dana asks Cindy, why was she acting so nervous. She asks her, was she alright. Cindy shook her head, to say everything was okay. Betty looked at Lil Ty. Then she made, Lil Ty understand that everything was cool now. Then Betty looks at Cindy. Lil Ty looks at the both, of them.

Dana did too. Betty made Cindy agree, that everything was fine. Dana didn't know what, where all of this was coming from. Still Dana was waiting for the outcome. Besides that, Cindy told Dana it was nice meeting her. Then Cindy offers Myesha some candy. Dana asks Myesha, what do say? Myesha looks at Cindy and says to her, thank you. Cindy gave Myesha a big bag of candy to take home.

Then she left them alone
with Lil Ty. Before Betty,
left Lil Ty and Dana, she
first, asks Dana about her
other nephew W.B... Dana
told her, he was alright.
Betty tells, Lil Ty to give
his uncle a chance. A
chance to get to know him.
Remember and always
know, your uncle loves you.
Just like I do. Dana looks
and waits for Lil Ty's
response to his aunt.
Lil Ty tell his aunt, he
loves her too.

Plus, he'll give his uncle another shot. So, they could get to know, one another better. Dana looks at him confused. But she didn't say much at this point of time. Dana let her son know, she was leaving. And her and Myesha would see him later, at home. Betty and Dana walks, out the store together. Once they were outside. They went their separate ways. Lil Ty went back to work.

That day, he was stacking
the shelves.

Chapter 10

As the years went by. Not only was Lil Ty changing. His brother W.B. grew in size, height, weight and in his stature. He was always husky built. Around his friends and family, he was known as Bear. The name was perfect for him. He resembles one, in size. As the years went by, the name stuck to him. Bear loved playing football. That was his thing.

All his coaches through the years, loved him. The way he played the sport. The way he played the game. He had a no joke attitude. Everyone knew that about him. Bear was more like Ty. When it came down to having and wanting power. Plain and simple, he wants and needs power. That's what made him a serious force, to be dealt with. When it came down to fighting. He wasn't the one to back down.

Or, the kind to run away from confrontations. The characteristics, he shared with his mother was overall, he was a good person. He cares about people. He was a very big and tall young man. He was a big dude that everyone wanted to be friends with. He was the type of person, who would give a friend, his shirt off his back, if they really needed it. Only if he cared for that person.

If you came across as an enemy, then you had a problem. And you got dealt with accordingly. The way he moved and acted, Dana knew how to deal with that, that's why she always kept him humble. Which worked, until he got older. Being humble and playing football, defined his childhood. Bear had his own crew of buddies. While, Lil Ty was somewhat, of a loner.

Bear was the opposite.
When it came down to
that. Bear had his own
team, which consisted of a
group of rough kids. And all
of them wanted to make a
name for themselves.
Basically, they were a
bunch of teenagers, from a
rough environment. Big
Bear was making a name
for himself, by himself, on
the streets. Everyone in
his neighborhood knew
Bear.

He was very young, built like a man, and very well respected. Lil Ty was tall and skinny. Bear was a little taller and huskier. Both were extremely bigger than their mother, Dana. When Ms. Medina would see her grandsons, she would always ask Dana, what she was feeding them boys? Because they were huge. Dana always laughs that off. She did agree with her mother.

Plus, she added the fact, the boys always eating. She felt like they were eating her of a house and a home. If you asked Myesha about it, she'll tell you that her big brothers were giants. Dana couldn't take them anywhere. Because everywhere they went, someone knew Bear. Especially, the girls. All the girls knew Bear. Dana always joked about the fact, with Bear.

She would ask him, if he was a superstar. Because he did have a fan club. He never gives his mother a response on that. He just smiles about it. He wasn't the type to tell his mother about everything. He wasn't telling her, what he did in the streets. Just like his father. He was not about to bring his dirt home with him. Where his mother and little sister lives at. Where he laid his head at.

He knew better than that. All his friends knew that as well. Whatever it was, you knew not to, knock on his door. You don't call him on the phone. You wait until you saw him, in person, on the streets. Even the old timers had nothing but love and respect for King Ty's son. He was well respected. Bear loves to hear about his father's street war stories. It made him proud to be his son.

When Lil Ty got his check from work. He opens his check envelope, he pulls out his check stub. He reads it. Then he reads it again. He was shocked by what he saw. His first thought was maybe it was some type of error. What made it even more shocking, when he went to the check cash. They cashed the check with no problems. He held his composure until he got a block away from the check cashing place.

Then a smile came on his face. Yet, still in disbelief. That he made so much money for the week. He never saw that kind of money, in his whole entire life. He went to work later, on that day. He asks one of co-workers how much did they make for the week. He told Lil Ty how much he made. Then he asks Lil Ty the same question. Lil Ty told him the same as he made.

If it was a mistake, he wasn't going to tell anyone or bring it up. He knew that for sure. The next day Saturday morning, he begins his day, by giving Bear a $100. At the time Bear was only 15 years old. Lil Ty and Bear went to the barber to get their haircuts. Afterwards, they headed to the mall. Lil Ty wanted to get some new sneakers and some new clothes.

He buys a pair of sneaker for Bear too. Bear wanted a new game for his game system. He used a portion of the hundred dollars Ty gave him. The two fellows, were beyond happy. Bear asks Lil Ty, where did he get all that money from? Lil Ty told him, he works hard for it. Bear didn't question his older brother again on that day, about that money. Bear knew it was more to it, than what he was saying.

He knew Lil Ty was full of it. Lil Ty wasn't being cheap with it. so, Bear went with the flow with everything. When Lil Ty got back home from the mall. He gave his mother 300 dollars. He gave her a hundred dollars for Myesha. A hundred towards the bills. And last, but not least, he gave his mother, Dana, a hundred dollars for herself. Dana notices while Ty was giving her the money, he had on new clothes.

She knew none of the clothes he had on, was cheap. Dana was happy to receive the money. Still, she didn't know where all, that money was coming from. What he gives her, she had already made it up in her mind, she was going to save for him. For a rainy day. Dana took it like this, with more hours of work, comes more money. Which results in bigger checks.

Lil Ty didn't tell his mother, how much he made, on his check. Lil Ty made a thousand dollars. Not a lot of money for an adult. For a 17-year-old, that was big business. That was huge amount to have. After spending a nice amount of money. He still had a nice amount left over. He kept his money in an old sneaker box. Which he places under his bed.

That was his little secret stash spot. Big Ty calls Betty from prison. She tells him, she had saw Dana. She got Dana's contact information. He was happy to hear about that. He asks for Dana's phone number. Betty gave it to him with no hesitation. He wanted to know how was Lil Ty doing at his job. She told him, Lil Ty was doing just fine.

In fact, she lets him know she did give Lil Ty, a little extra on his pay check. Ty was happy, Betty did what he asked her to do. Betty spoke about how much she gave Lil Ty on his check. She let it be known, she was giving him a thousand dollars on his weekly paycheck. That's what Big Ty wanted him to get. Not even Ty knew what his son will do with the money. He was, well aware of that.

He also, knew it would be up to his son, to do the right things with the money. Betty knows for sure, she did her part. Ty thanked his sister for everything, for all that she has does for him. Betty already knew what Ty was going to say next. He tells her, to take out some money for herself. She says thank bro., to her older brother. Ty understood he wanted to have his money undetected. That was his main, focus. He didn't need nor wanted, any heat being drawn to him. Ty told his sister, that one of these days, he'll give Dana a call. Soon, he'll be talking to Lil Ty as well. Ty ends his phone conversation with his sister. A couple of days later, he gives Dana a call. Dana knew sooner or later, Ty was going to call her. Ty call Dana out of the blue.

That day she wasn't expecting it. She knew what this call was going to be about. They haven't spoken to one another over 5 years. They had so much catching up to do. Both Dana and Ty had a lot questions and answers, that needed to be addressed. Where to being? Well let's see. Let's find out. Ty asks Dana about the kids. She tells him, they're doing fine.

He asks about his baby girl. She tells him, Myesha got very big. He tells Dana, that he knew what he had told her, to tell Myesha that he was dead. With that, being said, he still misses his little mommas, dearly. He admits that he had messed up big time. He made it clear, he let it be known, he really didn't want none of this. Nor, did he ask for any of it. His true intentions were to raise his family.

In the right way.
Unfortunately, with the
realization of his own
circumstances. His reality
dictates, that would not be
the case. So many
opportunities in this big old
world. Out of all the cards
that were dealt to him. He
felt like he had no good
ones. Not even one, in his
deck. He always felt, that
way. He vows, he didn't
want any of kids to be
dealt the same fate.

He was going to make sure, they didn't follow the same paths, that he chose to go down. He tells Dana, the kids would have no money problems in their future. He didn't go into details about it. All, he was saying about this was they will be well taken care of. Dana listened, but she didn't know what the hell he was talking about. Dana told him, what has happened to her and the kids since the last time they spoke.

She really didn't know what
he might have heard about
her. But it was important
to her that he heard it
from her. She tells him,
she had hit rock bottom.
He left her with three kids
to raise on her own. After
he went to prison. She
winds up with nothing. She
has no choice, but to go
into the shelter system.
She wasn't ashamed of
what she had to do, to
make sure her children had
a roof over their heads.

She wasn't ashamed about anything that has happened in her life. Because all that has happened, made her a stronger person. A better woman. All Ty could do, was listen to what Dana had to say. Questions were being answered. Before they were being asked. Dana told him, she was proud of the woman, she has become. Ty listens with full respect to the mother of his children.

He tells her, he was proud of Lil Ty. Proud of his son on so many levels. Just the fact, he was about to start the 12th grade, and he has a job. Because he wanted one. Both his parents had to acknowledge that. Time keeps on moving, no matter anyone's predicament. Time waits for no one. Time doesn't care about who you are. No one can stop the hands of time. It keeps on ticking away.

Ty asks about W.B., Dana tells him, Bear is an outstanding football player. And how big he was in size. Ty was pleased with what he was hearing. Dana and Ty were happy their kids were overall, good kids. Not perfect, but good. That's all they could hope and ask for. During the conversation, Dana slips in the fact, she was seeing someone. He asks her, were they serious?

She answers by saying, kind of, sort of. She thought about it. Then she flat out says, "Yes!", she was, and they were serious. Because deep down inside, she knew how she felt. She felt good, that she finally got that off her chest. Which made her feel, much better? Dana and Ty paused. Then Ty broke the ice. He tells her, he was happy for her. And he wishes her the best.

She could tell by the tone in his voice. That he was being sincere. He tells her, the guy she is seeing, better take good care of her, or else, he's going to deal with him, personally. They both laughed about that. Deep down inside, they both knew he was dead serious. Ty was just being, Ty...

Chapter 11

A couple of days later, Dana and Tanya have a nice conversation. Even though their friendship became estranged, distant. Not because of them. Because of life. No matter what, they always found time to check up, on one another. Dana asks Tanya about her 5-year-old daughter. Tanya tells her, that her daughter, Jamilah was doing just fine. She's be going to first grade in the fall.

Markie will be starting his third year in college. Dana was so proud of her God-son. Tanya went on to tell her, that Markie was working as an intern at a lawyer's office, here in the city. Dana was ecstatic to hear that. She was happy, he was doing big things with his life. Tanya asks about Lil Ty. Dana tells her, he works at a candy store. She tells her, Lil Ty was so happy, making his own money.

She mentions Bear, and his young football career. He was on the junior varsity squad. All Bear wants to do, is play football. Dana suggests, maybe they could meet up and go to one of Bear's football games. Tanya asks about Myesha, she answers simply with, Myesha is going to be Myesha. She's always on her daily missions. The mission to drive her crazy. They both laughed about that.

Tanya wanted to know, how things were going, with Dana and her guy friend. Dana let her know, they both were happy with one another. Besides that, nothing has changed. If anything, they got much closer. As Dana explains this to Tanya. Dana tells Tanya, she could actually, see herself with him, for the rest of her life. That news, just blew Tanya completely away, with that statement.

Tanya was bit happy for her, happier for herself, no less than for selfish reasons. Tanya asks her when was the last time, she heard from Ty. Dana changes the subject, she knew Tanya was just being extra nosy. Dana did tell Tanya, that candy store Lil Ty worked at, was owned by Ty brother, Stuy. Yet again, Tanya was shocked to hear that too. She had no knowledge of none of that.

Dana asks Tanya, why was she asking so much about Ty? It was Tanya's turn to stir away, from the real reason, why she was acquiring about that information. She tells Dana, she was just asking. Dana knew Tanya was silly and nosy like that. Tanya made sure, when Dana asks her, about the man in her life. She tells her long-time friend, that the man in her life got into a little trouble with the law.

He'll be home soon. Dana notices, Tanya didn't want to talk about that. So, she thought nothing of it. The two friends spoke for hours. Just like how they used to do it, way back when. Somethings never changes. Dana spent most Saturdays at her mother's place. Where she meets up with her sister Dameeka. As the ladies sat and talked, Dana brought up the fact, that Ty called her from prison.

She tells them, she had to let Ty know about the new man in her life. Ms. Medina and Dameeka paused. They both stops doing with they were doing. They gave Dana their complete, undivided attention. They wanted to hear about, how that went down. It sounded juicy to them. First, Ms. Medina asks her, when will they be meeting, this new love in her life. Ms. Medina went on to say, she's heard so much about this man.

Still she hasn't met this man yet. Her next question was to double check, what Dana had already stated earlier. She asks her again, did Ty know about this new-found relationship? Even her family was surprised at what she states next. She tells them, not only did Ty send them, his blessings. Plus, he was happy she found somebody that made her happy.

Both, Dameeka and Ms. Medina gave Dana a look, that expresses, the phrase, I hear that! Which was the reaction Ms. Medina had, seeing it, as hard to believe. She felt like, the reason why Ty was so calm about it, was because he was in prison. Let's see how he feels about it when he gets home. Then, you will really know. If he meant anything he was saying.

She wanted Dana, to understand, what someone says in prison, isn't always, how the person, may truly feel. Especially, when they have, to confront life changes, that they have no control over. They have tendencies to say, what they think a person, wants to hear, while their incarcerated. Dana understood where her mother was coming from. Dana also knew, she had to keep on, keeping on.

All she could go off of, was someone's word. That's all she could do. She wasn't trying over think it either. As the attention shifted. Dana and Ms. Medina notices, a mark under Dee's right eye. Where her cheap make-up was starting to wear off. Clearly, she had a black eye, hidden under her make-up. She didn't know how noticeable the bruise was. When they questioned her about it?

Dee did admit, that her and Dean, did get into a fight. She went on to say, she didn't believe, that he meant to do that to her. She tried to undermine the whole situation. By saying, they should have saw him. Because supposedly, she busted his lip. And he winded up with a swollen hand. She was so on the defensive, she wasn't realizing what she was saying.

Because none of what she was saying, sounded right. She tells them, that everything was alright now. She says it happened weeks ago, but you could tell it was a fresh wound. The main thing, was the safety of her and her daughter. Ms. Medina and Dana, knew it was way bigger than just that. The news of the day was, Dameeka telling them, that she was pregnant. Ms. Medina begins to question Dee.

She wanted to know how was her relationship going with that man. Dameeka tries to make a comparison of Dean and Ty. Quickly, she got shut down, on that one. Dana made it clear, Dean was no Ty. Ty never laid a hand on her. When they saw Dameeka got extremely over sensitive over the topic. They changed the subject. Not before Ms. Medina tells her daughter, Dameeka, no

matter what, her family
will always be here for her.
They will always have her
back. Plus, they all love
her. They just want what
was best for her. Dameeka
tells her mother and big
sister, she loves them too.
Who comes to moms late,
as usual, it was Mary
coming in the doors with
her kids. Mary didn't come
empty handed. She brought
dinner for everybody.
Myesha was happy to see
her aunt.

Ms. Medina was happy to see her children keeping up with traditions. Myesha receives a piece of chicken from her aunt Mary. She even did a little shake while, she ate her piece of chicken. Back to Ms. Medina, she was happy children, her kept up, with meeting up on Saturdays. Which was very important to her? Because, she understood, nowadays family can fall apart very easily.

The results, of not speaking, not seeing each other for years and years. Her belief was, family is supposed to always stick together. If not every weekend, at least once a month, should be set aside to spend time with family. So, they kids could actually grow up together. Learn and grow with one another. Family should be the rock, the foundation in one's life.

She thanks the man upstairs, that her children understood, what she was trying install, in them. She knew, she was truly blessed. Grateful and also thankful, to the highest, God.

Chapter 12

Tanya went to pay Ty a visit. Like she always did. She sits with him, she asks him, how was he doing? He tells her, he was chilling as always. She tells him, she couldn't wait until he comes home. He agrees. He does mention, he will be home, sooner than later. He only had a little bit to go. That's what he was telling her, she just looks at him. Because she knew he still had to do another 5 years of his sentence.

She wants him to understand, that when he gets out, he'll be coming home to her place to live with her. She puts him on to the fact, that she has spoken to Dana, the other day. She tells him about everything they spoke about. She mentions, Dana and her guy friend were getting closer than close. She paused. She was waiting and waiting for a response.

She got a response, she
wasn't expecting from him.
Ty tells her, he was happy
for Dana. Tanya tells him
about Lil Ty having to get a
job. She waits again.
Again, he really didn't have
too much to say about
that. What she didn't
know, was Ty already knew
about everything she was
bringing up. She told him,
she had a little surprise
for him when he gets
home, from prison.

Ty wanted to know about
that. He was interested in
what she has in store for
him. Tanya has mentioned
it to him before, maybe he
forgot about it. Ty was
confident, he felt like he
knew everything, that was
going on. He asks her
about her kids. She tells
him, they were doing good.
Tanya tells him, her
daughter couldn't wait to
see her daddy.

Ty had no reply, he thought nothing about what she was saying. She felt like it must of flew over his head. Because, he was sitting there, with no type of reaction. He asks her about her baby girl. he wanted to know, how old was she. Tanya tell him, her daughter was 5 years old, and she's about to turn 6. He tells her, that's how long he's been in the joint.

She looks at him, with a serious look on her face. That's when she said, "Exactly!" Ty stood there with his mouth wide opened. Tanya kisses him on his lips. He smells the sweet-scented perfume, she was wearing. She whispers in his ear, she tells him to think about that. He watches her, as she walks away. Ty remained there seated and in the state of shock.

The prison guards took him back to his jail cell. While sitting his jail cell, it finally hit him, when he put one and together. The news he just received, had him stunted. Tanya left him, with a bomb shell. Tanya left money for Ty, for commissary. He knew she'll be back in a couple of months, like she always did. A few months later, he calls Dana's place.

He asks, to speak to Lil Ty. Ty explains to Lil Ty the reasons behind his so-called hike in income. The extra money that Lil Ty thought no one knew about. Lil Ty didn't know where it had come from. Now he does. Ty tells Lil Ty, how he wants the extra money to be used. First, he tells him, that no one must know about the extra money, not even his mother.

The extra money on his check must always remain a secret. The conditions Ty gave Lil Ty was, he has to give his little brother and sister some of money. Lil Ty told his dad, that he already was giving them a hundred dollars apiece, when he gets paid every week. Ty likes what he was hearing. Ty liked the fact, that Lil Ty thought of this on his own.

Still, he felt like Lil Ty should give Bear 150 dollars, instead. After Lil Ty got over the complete surprise, of how the new-found money turned up. The question that was on Lil Ty's mind, has just been solved. Ty briefly explains to Lil Ty on what's about to come, the foundation. Ty asks Lil Ty, how was he doing? Was he looking out for his little brother and sister.

Was he respecting his mother? Lil Ty, just said "Yes!" to everything his father was saying. He took it, like his father was talking a bunch of jail mumbo, jumbo! Ty made sure, he made one thing clear, with Lil Ty. If he moves the way he wants him, to move. He will have so much money. Money beyond his wildest dreams. Ty tells his son, welcome to your life.

Which is my life. The
beginning of life, the life
of a King. Kings Ty-Bucks
Jr. is what he will always
be. This right here, and
right now, this will be our
little hidden secret. Again,
he says to him, not even
his mother must know about
this. Lil wouldn't have to
worry about a thing.
Everything will be covered
up. Ty told Lil Ty to take
care.

He'll be in contact soon.
Plus, he wants him, to
make sure, he sticks to the
game plan. If he does
that, everything else, will
fall into place...

(To Be Continue)

The story is not over.

Coming Soon

Medina #3